were totally sexually ine~~xp~~ ~~nun~~ or something.'

'Katie,' she had protested crossly, for once silencing her ebullient offspring, but later, alone in her bedroom, staring out of the window at the pretty Cheshire countryside which gave her so much inspiration for her work as an illustrator of children's books, she had been forced to concede that Katie had a point. She did tend to shrink away from unknown men. She was shy and rather withdrawn, unlike Katie, who, thank goodness, seemed to have much, much more self-confidence.

And as for her sexual experience... Remembering this last conversation with her daughter now, Hazel sighed to herself, automatically plumping up one of the pretty needlepoint cushions she had worked the previous winter, and settling it back on the old-fashioned brocade-covered chair, which had been her father's.

Even now after five years it still seemed odd to her to look at the chair and see it empty.

The stroke which had semi-paralysed her father four years after they had moved north from London had meant that in the last years of his life he had needed her in almost constant attendance. It had seemed a small enough way of repaying everything he had done for her and Katie.

Left alone with a four-day-old daughter at the age of forty-two, he couldn't have found it easy to bring her up alone. His wife, her mother, had died following complications with the birth. As he had once explained uncomfortably to her, neither he nor her mother had ever expected to have a child. They had married late in life, and her arrival had come as something of a shock.

Nevertheless he had loved her and done his best for her. His practice as a solicitor had demanded a great deal of his time, but he had been scrupulous about spending weekends with her, and a conscientious if somewhat over-protective housekeeper had been hired to take charge of the old Victorian house where she had grown up, and of her.

She had had a very protected and sheltered growing-up; a very lonely and isolated one in many ways, attending a very small girls' school from which she was picked up every day by Mrs Meadows, so that she was not given much opportunity to mingle with the other girls and make the friendships which might have drawn her out of her shell.

And then when she was sixteen she had met Jimmy.

He went to a nearby boys' school. He almost ran her down on his bicycle, and their friendship developed from there.

Jimmy was as ebullient and outward-going as she was shy and introverted, which was no doubt where Katie got her lovely laughing personality from.

Hazel adored and worshipped him, blindly following his lead in everything he suggested.

He wasn't a cruel or unkind boy; far from it, but he had a resilience which she lacked, and he was far, far too young to have the wisdom to look into the future and see the risks they were taking.

Looking back now, it seemed difficult for her to understand how at sixteen she could ever have believed she had fallen in love. With hindsight, she suspected that in Jimmy she had believed she had found the answer to her loneliness and that he was in many ways the friend, the brother, almost in fact the mother, she had never had.

Jimmy knew everything and everyone . . . Jimmy opened her eyes to so many things about life. Jimmy encouraged her to take advantage of her father's preoccupation with his work, to meet him illicitly in the evening . . . to spend long hours with him in the bedroom of the home he shared with his parents and brothers and sister.

The Garners were a large and very casual family. Ann Garner was an actress, Tony Garner a director; they were seldom at home, their five children left to the casual and careless discipline of a transient population of *au pairs* and relatives.

Ann Garner smiled at her in a preoccupied and busy fashion whenever she saw her in the house, but Hazel doubted if she even knew her name in those days and she was certainly not the kind of mother to make strenuous and exhaustive enquiries into her children's friendships. She was there, and she was accepted, and that was all there was to it.

But there was no point in trying to shift the blame, the responsibility on to Ann Garner's shoulders.

Hazel might have been naïve, she might have been stupid, but she did know what she was doing, did know the risks she was taking.

The first time Jimmy touched her, kissed her, she had been shocked—had withdrawn from him. She wasn't used to any kind of physical intimacy from others. Her father simply wasn't that kind of man, and Mrs Meadows had never encouraged what she termed 'soppiness'.

So she withdrew from him and Jimmy let her, watching her with curious, amused eyes. He was only twelve months older than her, but, in his knowledge of life, twenty years older.

'What's the matter? Don't you like it when I kiss you?' he asked her cheerfully.

She shook her head, flushing.

'That's because you don't know how to do it properly,' he told her with male assurance. 'You'll soon get to like it.'

And she soon did. She also liked the sensation of being physically close to him, of being held in his arms; of having someone special of her own in a way that her father and Mrs Meadows could never truly be hers.

The truth was that Jimmy filled a need in her life, healed a wound . . . gave her a special sense of identity and importance that made it impossible for her to think of refusing him anything. Even when that anything was the one thing she knew she ought to refuse.

But he was so tender, so coaxing. And even if, afterwards, she was forced to admit to herself that the experience had been more uncomfortable and embarrassing than anything else, at least she had the joy of knowing that she had pleased him. She knew that because he had told her so, kissing her with almost clumsy tenderness as he helped her to dress afterwards, and then taking her home on the

"You're cold. Perhaps we should go back."

Go back . . . If only Hazel could go back to before she had ever met Silas.

She had known him hardly more than twenty-four hours, and yet those twenty-four hours had changed her life irredeemably. Had changed her, showing her facets of her nature, of her innermost emotions and feelings, she had never known existed. If she had known more about him before she had met him, if she had had time to prepare herself . . . but she suspected that nothing she could have done could have protected her from the enemy that was within herself.

PENNY JORDAN was constantly in trouble in school because of her inability to stop daydreaming—especially during French lessons. In her teens, she was an avid romance reader, although it didn't occur to her to try writing one herself until she was older. "My first half-dozen attempts ended up ingloriously," she remembers, "but I persevered, and one manuscript was finished." She plucked up the courage to send it to a publisher, convinced her book would be rejected. It wasn't, and the rest is history! Penny is married and lives in Cheshire.

Penny Jordan's striking mainstream novel *Power Play* quickly became a *New York Times* bestseller. She followed that success with *Silver*, a story of ambition, passion and intrigue and *The Hidden Years*, a novel that lays bare the choices all women face in their search for love.

Books by Penny Jordan

Don't miss any of our special offers. Write to us at the following address for information on our newest releases.

Harlequin Reader Service
P.O. Box 1397, Buffalo, NY 14240
Canadian address: P.O. Box 603,
Fort Erie, Ont. L2A 5X3

PENNY JORDAN

A Forbidden Loving

Harlequin Books

TORONTO • NEW YORK • LONDON
AMSTERDAM • PARIS • SYDNEY • HAMBURG
STOCKHOLM • ATHENS • TOKYO • MILAN
MADRID • WARSAW • BUDAPEST • AUCKLAND

Harlequin Presents first edition November 1992
ISBN 0-373-11508-3

Original hardcover edition published in 1991
by Mills & Boon Limited

A FORBIDDEN LOVING

Printed in U.S.A.

CHAPTER ONE

HAZEL glanced nervously at the clock. Only another half-hour or so and they should be here. A pretty, dark-haired woman of thirty-six, she tried to hide her irritation as best she could when well-meaning people described her as 'petite' and exclaimed that she looked far too young to be her claimed age of thirty-six, never mind the mother of an almost-nineteen-year-old daughter into the bargain.

But that was exactly what she was, and it was as the mother of that very pretty, intelligent and popular nineteen-year-old that she was fretting anxiously about the arrangements she had made for Katie's first proper visit home since she had left for university at the end of the summer.

It had been all very well to gulp, hold her breath and exclaim as calmly as she could that there would be no problem when Katie had rung up three days ago and announced breezily that when she came home for the weekend she would not be alone, but would be bringing a friend with her. After all, she had had nineteen years in which to get used to the fact that Katie was an inveterate people collector, but what she hadn't expected was for Katie to continue excitedly, 'I know you're going to like Silas, Ma. He's a very special person and I can't wait for the two of you to meet.'

Her heart had plummeted immediately Katie had finished speaking, and, although she had successfully managed to hide it from her daughter, she had been overwhelmed by a sharp sense of fear.

And yet Katie had had boyfriends before, of course; several of them in fact; gangly, sometimes spotty young men, who blushed and stammered, or adopted an unwittingly touching and amusing male machismo which sat very uncomfortably on their as yet still boyish shoulders. But this time it was different. This time... This time she felt all the apprehension and alarm of a mother who felt that her child was threatened in some way.

She had sensed just from the way Katie spoke his name that this Silas was important to her. Too important... She gave a tiny shiver, frowning unseeingly around her small sitting-room.

She could never really understand those women who claimed that their teenage daughters were their best friends. She felt far too great a sense of responsibility and awareness of life's cruelties and unkindnesses ever to relax her maternal vigilance enough to make *that* claim.

She hoped she wasn't a possessive mother. All through Katie's growing years she had worked hard at making sure that Katie never became distanced from her peers or from other adults, or suffered the kind of aloneness and isolation which she had suffered as a child.

The trouble was that Katie had been so vague about this Silas Jardine, and she had not liked to question her too deeply. All she knew about him was that Katie had met him at the university and that she was sure that he and her mother were going to get on like a house on fire. It sounded very ominous to Hazel. She had been all too maternally aware that, behind her insouciance and bright chatter, Katie was hiding something.

Biting her bottom lip, Hazel checked round the sitting-room again.

A warm fire burned in the grate, and logs were heaped up in the basket beside the fire, logs which had been supplied by Tom Rawlins from the farm, about whom Katie was always teasing her by describing him as her adoring swain.

It was true that she and Tom occasionally went out for a meal or to see a show. He was a widower with two grown-up children; she was... Well, she was the mother of an almost grown-up daughter and it was only natural that they should have things in common. But that was as far as any relationship between them went.

Fortunately Tom was far too gentlemanly to make the kind of sexual demands she so dreaded and detested receiving.

It had shocked her three years ago, when Katie had coolly announced that it was high time that her mother stopped behaving as though she ought to be punished and despised simply because she had given birth to an illegitimate child, and started feeling proud of herself instead for all that she had done for that child.

'Ma, every time a man looks at you, you shrink visibly. You're a very attractive woman. Everyone says so, and I for one certainly wouldn't object if you decided to provide me with a stepfather, providing of course that I liked him.'

'Well, for your information, I have no intentions of doing any such thing,' Hazel had retaliated sharply.

'Why not? You should think about it,' Katie had told her smartly, adding critically, 'Just look at you. As long as I can remember it's just been you, and me, and of course Gramps. I *know* it must have been awful for you, losing Dad like that in such an awful accident and then finding out about me. But I don't see why just because of that you've got to spend the rest of your life hiding away from men. You can't get pregnant just by smiling at them, you know,' she had added with typical teenage scorn. 'You can't want to spend the rest of your life alone. With Gramps gone...'

'It's all right,' Hazel had told her shakily but drily. 'If you're worried about having a geriatric parent on your hands cramping your style, I assure you that you need not be.'

That had made Katie laugh and the subject had been dropped, but Katie had resurrected it with uncomfortable frequency as the time drew nearer for her to leave home and go to university.

'You're so young, Ma,' she had expostulated more than once. 'Men fancy you. I've seen the way they look at you, but you... Well, you behave like— like a shrinking virgin.'

When Hazel had flushed and protested, Katie had grimaced and added, 'Look at yourself now and you'll see what I mean. Anyone would think you new motorbike which he had bought himself with his birthday money.

His parents had been away for his birthday, his mother touring in the first run of a new play, his father directing a TV movie in Greece, but they had both sent him cards, and there had been a generous cheque to go into his bank account.

That cheque had bought the motorbike of which he was so proud. A huge, powerful thing which privately Hazel didn't like, but which she was far too loyal to criticise. Jimmy loved the bike; she loved him; therefore the bike was wonderful.

As he dropped her off outside her house that Saturday afternoon, he teased her by dropping a quick kiss on her lips before she could turn her head to look anxiously towards the house, terrified that her father might have seen them.

Jimmy was vastly amused by this fear of hers that her father might see them together.

'What if he does?' he asked her, genuinely curious. 'Does it matter? Has he forbidden you to go out with me?'

She was forced to shake her head. Boys and whether she might or might not go out with them was simply a subject that could not be raised with her father. The thought of her even beginning to do so made her quail, and yet her father was not overly strict, and was certainly not unkind. Just the opposite; he was gentle, if somewhat remote. So why did she feel it was so impossible to tell him about Jimmy? She had no real idea—she just knew that it was, just knew with instinctive feminine wisdom that, to her father, she was still very much a little girl and that that was how he wished her to stay.

Even though he had promised to telephone her, she didn't hear from Jimmy that evening, nor all of the next day, and it wasn't until she was back at school on Monday that she heard the gossip running round the playground.

Jimmy was dead... Killed in an accident when he had lost control of the new motorbike of which he was so proud. His sister wasn't at school.

A note had been sent to the headmistress hurriedly explaining the facts. Jimmy's parents had been sent for... Everyone who ought to know what had happened had been informed—apart from her.

Somehow or other she made it through the day, going home to be violently sick in her bathroom, unable to take in what had happened... unable to accept that she would never see Jimmy again.

She didn't go to the funeral—didn't feel able to intrude on the family in their grief, even though she visited the cemetery the following day herself to lay a small floral tribute there and to say a special prayer for him.

It wasn't until almost four months after Jimmy's death that she realised she was pregnant and even then it had taken someone else, one of the teachers at school, to gently question her and elicit the truth.

To their credit, both families took the news of her pregnancy very well, and when she announced that she wanted to keep her baby, Jimmy's baby, there were no attempts at forcing her to do otherwise.

Even so, despite his kindness and concern, she was sensitively aware that she had shocked her father, and guiltily she felt that she had somehow let him down; that her behaviour had not been what he had expected in his daughter.

Her guilt was intensified when, within a month of Katie's birth, he announced that he was selling his practice and retiring and that the three of them would be moving away from London.

Despite the fact that he never once reproached her, even despite the fact that he had already told her that she was still his daughter and that her place and her child's would still be under his roof, she knew intuitively that it was because he felt embarrassed and let down in having an illegitimate grandchild that he felt compelled to make these changes in their lives.

But she was still barely seventeen, and a very young seventeen at that, far too young to even think of leaving home and living by herself even if she had the means to do so.

There could be no question of her continuing at school, of course, and once Katie was born she had no real desire to do so. Her little daughter became the focus of her whole world.

When Mrs Meadows, outraged to learn that she was pregnant, had handed in her notice, she had taken over the running of the house, surprised to discover how much she had learned from the older woman, who had not been above insisting that she helped her out with the chores. The housekeeper, before she had left, had told Hazel in no uncertain terms how fortunate she was in having so kind and generous a father.

Phrases such as 'if you had been my child', and 'your father, poor man, I don't know how he can bear the disgrace', had been freely bandied about and after Mrs Meadows had gone Hazel had sworn passionately to herself that from now on she would do everything she could to make amends to her father for all the pain she was causing him.

Quite why her father chose to move to Cheshire, he never actually explained, but Hazel was beyond caring where they went.

As it happened, she liked the quiet Cheshire village with its pretty fields and distant views of Alderley Edge and the Welsh hills, but when her father suggested rather awkwardly that she might prefer to pretend to people that she and Jimmy had actually been married, she uncomfortably shook her head.

Not even to please her father could she live that sort of a lie. She knew now that there would always be those who would condemn and vilify her for Katie's birth, just as there would always be those who would reach out to her with understanding and compassion, generously accepting that Katie's conception had been a pitiful accident rather than the result of a depraved lifestyle.

But it wasn't until Katie was just five years old that she fully realised just how sensitive her father was about her unmarried state.

Since it was something he never referred to, she had hoped that he, like herself, had come to accept that, while Katie's conception was not the best thing that could have happened to a sixteen-year-old, Katie herself was a beloved bonus who more than made up for her mother's disgrace in conceiving her. But one afternoon, when she was collecting Katie from school, she fell into conversation with another parent who was also collecting his child.

Robert Bolton was an outwardly pleasant man, a few years older than she was herself, whom she understood to be divorced from his wife, and who had custody of two young sons.

The thought that he might possibly misconstrue their few moments of idle conversation outside the school gates never even crossed Hazel's mind, never mind the thought that, because of her unmarried state, because Katie was illegitimate, he might jump to the assumption that, having already had one lover, she might welcome another.

But when he turned up at the house and asked her out, her father was so disapproving and so upset that even though she had no intention of accepting the invitation she felt compelled to ask her father why he objected so strongly.

At first his response was evasive.

She had to be careful, he told her uncomfortably. It wouldn't do to have people gossiping.

'Gossiping about what?' she asked him, genuinely not understanding.

For the first time that she could remember, he lost his temper with her.

Did she not remember that she had an illegitimate child? he demanded tersely. Did she not remember that the disgrace of that had driven them away from London? But that kind of disgrace could never be totally evaded. People talked, people knew... If men started calling here at the house for her...

And then Hazel understood, and quietly but firmly she closed the door in her heart which might have led to an adult relationship with a man. The kind of relationship which might ultimately have brought her true sexual and emotional fulfilment as a woman, the kind of relationship she had sometimes yearningly daydreamed of, the kind of relationship she had envied other women sharing with their men, but which she now understood could never be for her.

In her father's eyes she would always be branded by Katie's birth. Who knew how many other men might feel the same way, might feel that she was sexually available and easy, because of that?

Because *that* was what her father had been trying to say to her, even though he had been too embarrassed to put it quite so plainly. As the mother of an illegitimate child, she had a reputation. Men approaching her would only be doing so *because* of that reputation, because they wanted sex from her. And even if that was not true, she could not risk hurting and upsetting her father again by inviting what he would see as speculation and gossip about her morals.

She reminded herself that she was very fortunate, very lucky in that her father was prepared so generously to house and support her. That without that support her precious Katie would never have had the lifestyle she now did. A lovely home, the security that was provided by her grandfather's money, the lovely surroundings in which she was growing up. Without her father to provide these things for them, their lives would have been so very different. Hazel wasn't sixteen any more. She knew quite well how difficult life was for other single mothers, how very fortunate she was. The least she could do was to repay her father by respecting his wishes. And, after all, were they so difficult to live by? All right, so there was no man in her life, no lover, no husband... but she had her precious Katie. She had her father, she had her lovely home, and she was slowly making new friends.

And if sexually she was still as unawakened as she had been when Katie was conceived, well, was she really so very bothered? She could barely remember what it had felt like when Jimmy made love to her. What she *could* remember was that she had not been particularly enthralled by the experience; that she had not had a physical desire to repeat it. What she had enjoyed, though, was the closeness it had brought between her and Jimmy, the tenderness with which he had kissed her afterwards. But these were very dim memories now, the memories of a child, not a woman... and if the price she must pay for Katie's security and her father's peace of mind was her own celibacy, well, so be it.

Over the years she had kept in contact with Jimmy's family, who had all accepted Katie as his daughter. She and Katie had spent several holidays with Jimmy's mother, who was now divorced from Jimmy's father, and as the rest of the family grew up, married and produced children, Hazel made sure that Katie knew her aunts and uncles and her cousins.

She didn't want Katie to suffer as she had done through being too isolated and over-protected. She didn't want Katie to repeat her mistakes, to yearn, without knowing she did so, for contact with her peers to such an extent, to yearn for love so much that she mistook a healthy male teenager's natural desire to express his sexuality for that love and responded to it with the same disastrous results as she, Hazel, had done.

But Katie *wasn't* her, as Katie herself had gently pointed out to her when she had first started going out on dates. Guiltily Hazel had acknowledged that she was glad in many ways that her own father had died before Katie had reached this stage in her life, because she would not have wanted him to inflict on Katie the mental and emotional taboos he had inflicted on her. It would not be right for her own sins to be visited upon her precious daughter. All she could do was to pray that Katie was strong enough, mature enough, happy enough not to need to make an intense emotional commitment to a member of the opposite sex until she was old enough to handle any potential sexual consequences.

So far she had been lucky, she acknowledged, restlessly smoothing another cushion. So far none of Katie's relationships with the opposite sex had been remotely serious. But she herself had an almost morbid fear of Katie repeating her mistakes.

She didn't want Katie's freedom, Katie's joy, Katie's life curtailed in the way in which her own had been curtailed. For Katie, she wanted everything she had not had herself.

For Katie, she wanted the very best that there was: a good education; the strength and self-confidence that came from knowing she could support herself.

A sad smile crossed her face. Art had been her own best subject at school. She had once hoped to go on to college to study it further, but Katie's arrival had put paid to that. Nevertheless, she *had* found a way of using that talent, even if she had discovered it rather late in life.

After her father's death, and because she had felt so guilty, so uncomfortable in the now empty house during the day, she had started taking adult education classes.

Her art teacher had been so impressed with her skill that she had recommended her to an agency she knew who specialised in supplying illustrators for writers.

For the last two years, Hazel had worked exclusively for one particular writer, supplying all the illustrations for her very popular younger children's books.

Had she discovered this talent when she was younger, who knew what might have happened. Given the freedom of financial independence, she might have felt able to go out more, to meet people, to perhaps even meet a man... But then what would have happened to her father? After his stroke he had never fully recovered. He had needed her then as she had needed him after Katie's birth and she had always been grateful that fate had given her the opportunity to show him her love and her gratitude.

Now financially and physically she was free, but she *was* thirty-six years old: far too old to be thinking of romance, of love. And besides these days when she looked around, when she looked properly at the men around her, she saw with distaste that many of them, while smiling and flirting with women who were not their partners, were hurting those partners and seemed not to care that they were doing so. That many of them were weak and vain; that others were like dependent children, greedily taking everything their women had to offer and giving precious little back; and she had come to the conclusion that, for every happy couple she knew, she knew three who were not, and that perhaps after all fate had not truly been punishing her in denying her the right to her sexual and emotional fulfilment as a woman.

The very firm distance she had initially learned to keep between herself and the male sex, to please her father, had become a defence mechanism behind which she retreated for safety, causing Katie to tell her sternly that she was behaving more like a woman of seventy than one of half that age.

'You're really attractive, Mum,' Katie had told her fondly. 'Far too attractive to be living on your own.'

'Hasn't it occurred to you that I might want to live alone?' Hazel had retaliated. 'Lots of women do. Take Jessy Finlay, for instance.'

Jessy was a forty-year-old redhead, who owned a small cottage on the outskirts of the village, and who worked as a freelance reporter for a local TV station. She was outrageously extrovert, and very popular with all the local men, if somewhat less popular with their wives.

'Jessy might live alone, but she does *not* sleep alone,' Katie had informed her mother brutally, softening a little to add quietly, 'It's not natural, Ma. I know there isn't any man in your life. I know you don't have a discreet lover tucked away somewhere. Has there ever been anyone apart from Dad?'

Much as she longed to tell her that that was none of her business, Hazel had found herself admitting that there had not. What Katie did not seem to realise and what she had no intention of telling her was that she herself was the result of her own single and unmemorable sexual experiment. And, uncomfortable though it made her feel to contemplate it, Katie at eighteen probably had a good deal more sexual experience than she had at nearly twice that age.

Although she had always been scrupulous about making sure that Katie was as well informed on sexual matters as she could be, Hazel had always felt lamentably aware of her own inability to convey to her daughter that, exciting though sexual experimentation might be in one's teens, true fulfilment, true sexual pleasure was something one could only truly appreciate with maturity.

All she had felt able to say to Katie was that she must always do only what felt right for her; that it was her own feeling of self-worth, her feeling of self-respect that was important, far more important than giving in to peer pressure or the importunings of some callow boy.

But how could she discuss with her daughter adult sex, adult emotions, a woman's emotions, a woman's needs, when she herself had no knowledge of these things?

Since Katie had left school at the beginning of the summer, Hazel had gradually begun to feel that she was the child and her daughter the parent. Katie now seemed so grown-up, so mature, so much better able to handle herself than Hazel.

Hazel had watched in awe and pride as Katie parried the over-fulsome compliments of the older men among their acquaintance, who were suddenly claiming that she was becoming very grown-up, and very, very attractive. Firmly but pleasantly Katie had let them know that she considered their interest to be avuncular. Firmly she had made it clear that she was not interested in their heavy-handed flirtation. And she was just as adept at dealing with her own peers.

Hazel had seen her off for university with a heavy heart, acknowledging that the child had gone and a woman had taken her place. She was so proud of her daughter. Proud of all that she was and all that she would be, and she had prayed desperately that Katie would get safely through university and launch herself in her chosen career before she fell deeply in love.

Now it seemed as though in making those prayers she, her mother, had brought down on her the very fate she had wanted her to escape.

True, Katie had said nothing about being in love with this Silas. Silas...what sort of name was that? It was far too theatrical, far too...too male. But the very way she said his name, the very hesitation in her voice, the very fact that she, Hazel, her mother was so acutely aware of these things, made Hazel desperately anxious to make the acquaintance of this man who, it seemed, had become so important to her daughter. And equally it made her extremely reluctant to get to know him, as though in doing so she was acknowledging his importance in Katie's life.

It wasn't just maternal jealousy either; it wasn't that she resented someone else becoming more important to Katie than she was herself...well, not entirely.

Guiltily she tugged at her own swollen bottom lip.

Upstairs two immaculate and comfortable bedrooms were waiting for their arrival.

Two bedrooms. Katie would sleep in her own bedroom, of course. Her *friend*, this Silas...

Gnawing on her swollen lip, Hazel stared unseeingly across the pretty sitting-room, for once not seeing the charm of its exposed timbers, its low ceilings, and its deep stone-framed windows.

The house was old, very old, and she had fallen in love with it the first time she had seen it. She suspected that if her father hadn't been in such a hurry to move them out of London he would have waited until something more modern came on the market, but as it was he had bought this pretty half-timbered Cheshire farmhouse with its large gardens and its wonderful aspects over the surrounding countryside, and gradually over the years Hazel had put her stamp on it, had brought it to life with all her gentleness and artistic skill, so that people coming into it for the first time caught their breath in pleasure as they studied its colour-washed rooms with their faded chintzes and brocades, its air of homeliness and comfort, its gentle warming welcome to everyone who walked into it.

Perhaps she should have taken hold of her courage and asked Katie outright if she expected this Silas to share her room, her bed. But then Katie's room still only had the small single bed she had all through her teens.

That was no excuse, she told herself severely. The house had five bedrooms and two bathrooms. The room she had made up for Katie's friend was the smallest of these, right next door to her own room. It had a tiny dormer window, and a polished wooden floor. It also had a large double bed. All the rooms apart from Katie's and her own did, and she could hardly have moved out of her own room, not without causing Katie to make some comment.

So what would she do if Katie gaily announced that she would move into the spare-room with their guest for the duration of his visit? What would she do if this Silas chose to insist that Katie show her mother just how committed she was to him by sleeping with him?

Hazel had heard enough horror stories from other parents, other mothers confronted with just this sort of situation to feel more than mere apprehension. It wasn't that she didn't want to admit that her daughter was an adult, a woman. Of course she knew, of course she accepted . . . but it was one thing to accept that Katie was old enough to have a sexual relationship with someone, and quite another to be forced to witness that relationship, to be forced to have all her fears and anxieties revived right under her nose. It was bad enough worrying about Katie when she couldn't see what she was doing . . .

If only they would arrive. Or, even better, if only they would ring and say they'd changed their minds. She was dreading meeting him, dreading it . . .

But for Katie's sake she would have to pretend that she was happy for her. She would have to pretend that she liked him.

Stop it, she warned herself. He's probably a very nice boy. He's probably just as much in love as Katie is. He's probably just as vulnerable, and he's also probably got a mother somewhere dreading meeting Katie as much as I'm dreading meeting him.

CHAPTER TWO

SURELY they couldn't be much longer? About four o'clock, Katie had said. Now it was almost five. Hazel's stomach knotted and churned. What if there'd been an accident? History repeating itself—Katie dying as her father had died...

Once again she had to stop herself from allowing her imagination to run away with her.

She had prepared Katie's favourite supper, including a pie made from their own Bramley apples. She had enough carefully stored to take her over Christmas and into the new year.

Secretly she had been looking forward to Christmas, to having Katie home, treasuring the thought of it like a child with an illicit hoard of sweets, because she knew that after this first term, after this first year, Katie would make her own friends and would naturally want to spend future holidays with them. So deep in her heart lurked the knowledge that this coming Christmas could be their last together. Now she wondered, shivering in the chill of the thought, if she would be expected to share Christmas with this Silas, or, even worse, if he would take Katie away from her completely, if the two of them would spend their Christmas somewhere alone, while she...

As she heard the sound of a car drawing up outside, her stomach muscles tensed and she froze, and then forced herself to walk as calmly as she could towards the front door.

As she passed the mirror hanging over the fireplace, she glanced surreptitiously into it. What would he see, this Silas, who threatened her peace of mind so much? She frowned at her own reflection, wondering if he would notice or even care that she and Katie shared the same heart-shaped face, and the same slightly almond-shaped eyes, but where hers were an uncertain, hesitant greeny-brown—hence her name—Katie's were a brilliant laughing blue, just as her curls were mere brunette, where Katie's were glossily and extravagantly black.

Katie's colouring, like her height, came from her father, but they shared the same fine bone-structure, the same delicacy of wrist and ankle. One thing she did envy Katie, though, was her height. Hazel hated being so small, barely five feet two, and so slender with it that there were still occasions when people called at the house and found her dressed in jeans and a T-shirt working in the garden and, seeing her from the back, made the mistake of assuming that she was still a child.

Perhaps if she wore her hair in a different style, but it was so curly and untameable that there was little she could do with it other than to have it go its own wayward way.

The front door of the house was wooden and solid. She could see nothing through it as she unbolted and then opened it, but already in her mind's eye she could see her daughter: laughing, exuberant, flinging herself into her arms, and almost knocking her over as she did so—only when she did open the door, there was no sign of Katie.

Instead a man was climbing out of the car parked on her drive, smiling slightly at her as he acknowledged her presence.

Disappointment mingled with relief. Whoever this man was, he could not be Katie's precious Silas. He was too old, for one thing, closer to forty-five than twenty-five.

He was probably a stranger who had lost his way. Certainly he wasn't anyone she knew she had ever met. Had she done so she would have been bound to remember him. He was far too attractive, far too male for any woman to be able to forget. Her heart gave a tiny unsteady thump as her brain acknowledged what her senses had already registered; namely that this stranger walking towards her was an extremely virile and masculine man, whose casual attire of well-worn jeans and soft denim shirt revealed a body packed hard with muscle and male strength.

Hazel could feel the most odd sensation burgeoning into life in the pit of her stomach. She wanted to wrap her arms tightly around herself as though doing so would control this strange, unnerving feeling.

'Miss Partington?' he queried, coming towards her.

His voice was deep and pleasant. The way he spoke her name made Hazel feel faintly dizzy. *Her* name. How had he known her name?

'Er—yes. I'm afraid I don't know...'

He was extending his hand towards her, so that she automatically reciprocated the gesture, her eyes registering the shock caused by the brief physical contact between them. What was the matter with her? She had shaken a man's hand before, for heaven's sake.

Feeling thoroughly flustered, she looked uncertainly at him.

'I'm sorry. I haven't introduced myself.' He smiled at her. 'I'm Silas Jardine. I dropped Katie off in the village. She said something about wanting to buy something. She told me not to wait, said she might be a little while, and told me to come and introduce myself. She said something about wanting to catch up on some gossip. It really is kind of you to put me up like this.'

Hazel wasn't listening any longer. She was staring at him in shocked disbelief.

This man could not be Katie's Silas. This man could not be Katie's *boyfriend*. Boyfriend! This was no boy. Outrage mingled with her shock. How could he stand there, glibly carrying on a conversation with her, when all the time he must know how shocked she was, how stunned, how... yes, how disbelieving that he could...? That he could what? Love her daughter? She caught herself up on the thought. What was that feeling beginning, like a cold, sharp dagger in her middle? That wasn't maternal protectiveness, was it? That was... That was...

It was nothing, she told herself quickly. It was nothing at all, and it certainly wasn't an un-

comfortable and impossible stab of something
almost approaching betrayal.

Her smile had turned to a frown now, as her
shock registered all too plainly on her face. She
could almost feel him withdrawing from her, dis-
tancing himself from her with cool reserve. Panic
clawed at her. This was a situation she simply could
not deal with, did not know how to deal with. When
she had envisaged Katie's Silas, she had envisaged
a younger man—a much younger man. This man
was far too old for Katie. Far, far too old.

She started to tremble, suddenly feeling in-
credibly weak and sick. Tears of shock blurred her
eyes, causing her to clench her jaw and hurriedly
blink them away.

'I'm sorry. I seem to have given you something
of a shock.'

He was too astute, saw too much, and suddenly
she was desperately frightened of him. What if he
should sense her anger, her shock, her disgust, her
outrage, and punish her for them by trying to turn
Katie against her? Once she would have said that
could never happen but then once she would have
said that Katie would never have any need in her
life that would lead her to imagine herself in love
with a man old enough to be her father.

'Look, I think we'd better get you inside. Katie
warned me that you hate people saying you look
fragile, but . . .'

Katie had told him *that*. What else had she told
him? Hazel wondered achingly as she stepped back
into the hall, fighting to get her shock under
control.

She hated him, she decided fiercely as he followed her inside. She hated him already. How could she not do when she looked at him and saw in his face, in his eyes, all his years of living, and then compared those years, that maturity with Katie's youth?

She knew all about men like him. Men who were too insecure to love women who could match them in terms of age and experience. Their vanity led them to feed off youth, like leeches. Oh, yes, she knew the type all right and she despised it, but she had never, ever envisaged that Katie would fall prey to such a man, no matter how good-looking he might be—and this man was certainly that, she acknowledged grudgingly, trying to ignore the *frisson* of sensation that danced over her skin as she looked up and discovered that she was being studied with gravely thoughtful interest by Silas Jardine's disturbingly perceptive cool grey eyes.

'Are you sure you're all right?' he asked her quietly. 'Katie——'

Whatever he had been about to say was forgotten as the front door was flung open, and Hazel heard her daughter calling out cheerfully, 'Ma, Ma... where are you?'

'Noisy lot, aren't they, the young?' Silas Jardine remarked easily as she hurried towards the door. His comment made her check and turn to give him an indignant look. What on earth was he trying to do, aligning himself with her? Did he honestly think that she was stupid enough to fall for such a ploy or that it would endear him to her, or incline her to accept him as her daughter's lover?

The sickening sour scald of revulsion that burned through her at the thought turned her indignation to self-disgust, and she turned away from him quickly before her face could betray her.

She was becoming frighteningly aware that if he chose to do so this man could drive a wedge between her and her beloved daughter that might never be removed.

Hopefully, please God, there would come a time when Katie would open her eyes and see him for what he undoubtedly was; a forty-odd-year-old man who was bolstering his ego, his machismo by feeding off her youth. And when that time came he would no longer have a place nor a role in her life, but by then Hazel suspected that it would be too late to heal the rift which he could cause between them.

She would have to be careful, so very careful not to betray to Katie how shocked and distraught she felt, she acknowledged as she hurried into the hallway and was immediately taken hold of and swung off her feet as Katie gave her an enthusiastic hug.

'You've lost weight,' she scolded her mother maternally as she set her back on the floor and studied her critically, and then, turning to Silas who had also come out into the hall, she demanded happily, 'Isn't she everything I told you she was?' Without waiting for a response, she turned back to Hazel and grinned at her.

'He wouldn't believe me when I told him I had a mother who looked like a teenager and not a fully grown-up one at that,' Katie teased.

To her intense mortification, Hazel discovered that she was actually blushing, something she'd thought she had successfully got under control years ago.

Katie laughed and teasingly tousled her curls, telling her, 'I stopped off in the village to buy this. I've got you a proper present, of course, but I thought we could have this tonight to celebrate.'

When Hazel didn't say anything, she added in a more gentle voice, 'You didn't think I'd forgotten, did you, Ma? I shan't embarrass you in front of Silas by mentioning the fact that you're thirty-six years old today.'

'Katie!' Hazel expostulated weakly. To tell the truth, she herself had almost forgotten that it was her birthday in the anxiety of worrying about her daughter, but now that Katie had reminded her of the date she wished that she hadn't. It wasn't the thought of adding another year to her age that bothered her. No, it was the quiet, assessing way that Silas Jardine was continuing to study her that made her feel so uncomfortable. His mouth twitched a little as she removed the bottle of champagne from Katie's exuberant grasp, and told her as firmly as she could, 'Katie, you know quite well that I gave up celebrating my birthday years ago.'

'*You* may have done so, but that doesn't mean that the rest of us have to follow suit,' Katie informed her, adding, 'What time are we eating, Ma? I'm starving. I wanted to stop off on the way, but Silas said there was no way he was going to poison his insides with the stuff they serve in motorway fast food outlets. He's even worse than you,' she added grumbling, while Hazel gave a doubtful look in Silas's direction, wondering how he was taking this criticism.

A little to her surprise he seemed more amused than annoyed, his manner more that of an indulgent uncle than a passionate lover. It seemed oddly out of keeping, because this man *would* be a passionate lover. A tiny thrill of shock tingled down her spine, a sensation almost of actually being touched. She shivered under it, sensitively cringing from the intimacy of her own thoughts. Thoughts she had no right to have, no right at all. Silas Jardine was her *daughter's* lover and not...

Not what? she asked herself shakily. Not an exceptionally virile and male man, whose simple presence in her home was making her feel as nervous and on edge as though *she* were the one who was the teenager?

It was all his fault. If he had arrived, as he had been supposed to do, with Katie, she would never... he would not... She bit her bottom lip hard.

What on earth was the matter with her? She had seen good-looking men before, talked to them, spent time with them, without going to pieces like this.

And she *was* going to pieces. She only had to look at him and she could feel herself disintegrating inside.

This is ridiculous, she told herself firmly. She had to pull herself together. What on earth was happening to her? Surely—she could feel herself going hot with self-disgust at the thought—surely she wasn't about to turn into one of those dreadful women who in middle age seemed to develop an embarrassing need to prove themselves by flirting very desperately and very obviously with their daughters' boyfriends?

Desperately she tried to concentrate on what Katie was saying to her, telling her nervously, 'Well, I've made your favourite for supper: roast beef with all the trimmings and apple pie.'

She couldn't bring herself to look at Silas, and so, instead, she said to Katie, 'I should have checked with you that your friend—er—Mr...doesn't mind such plain fare...'

When she had envisaged Katie's 'friend', she had been thinking in terms of a much younger man with far less sophisticated tastes than the very obvious man of the world who was now addressing her, telling her smoothly, 'Please call me Silas—and to tell the truth a home-cooked meal will be rather a treat for me.'

Katie gave him a dancing look of amusement.

'Don't listen to him, Ma. He's got females queuing feet deep, just longing to offer him all the home comforts.'

She could just bet he had, Hazel reflected acidly to herself, and she doubted that it was just their cooking that they wanted him to sample.

In Katie's shoes, she suspected that she would have felt far more concerned than her daughter obviously did.

Despite the fact that there was nothing remotely lover-like about their behaviour to one another, Katie must be very, very sure indeed of his feelings for her if she could afford to treat the subject so lightly. She looked at her daughter, rather wonderingly and wistfully. In Katie's shoes, she doubted that she could have exhibited such self-confidence.

It was all very well for her to tell herself that he was a very lucky man to have the love of someone as precious and wonderful as her Katie, but Katie was, after all, not quite nineteen years old, while he... Oddly enough, he didn't look like the kind of man who needed to bolster his ego by parading a much, much younger girl on his arm, but then neither had she ever imagined that Katie would look for a relationship with a man so much older than herself, a man more suited in age to be her father than her lover.

Guiltily she wondered if it was her fault; if it was because *she* had failed to provide Katie with a father that her daughter had now made the dangerous mistake of falling for this man.

'How long will supper be, Ma?' Katie pressed her.

'Oh, not long—about an hour.'

'Great. I'll just take Silas upstairs and show him his room and then I'll come down and give you a hand and we can have a natter. Which room is he in, by the way?'

In the shock of discovering how much older than Katie her lover was, Hazel had almost forgotten her anxiety over their sleeping arrangements.

Now they came back to her abruptly, and she discovered that it was impossible for her to look at Silas as she told Katie uncertainly, 'I've put your—

er—Mr...er—Silas in the spare-room; the one next to mine.'

Why oh why was she blushing when she said that? And why of all things was she so intimately and so wrongly suddenly mentally presented with a very disturbing and highly visual image of Silas's broad-shouldered and very male form lying beneath the covers of her spare bed, his skin tanned and sleek, his...?

She swallowed visibly, weakly trying to dismiss such erotic and unwanted thoughts. Heavens, the man might not even have a tan, never mind...

'The nursery, you've put Silas in my old nursery.' Katie grinned. 'If you can't sleep, Silas, you'll be able to entertain yourself reading my old books. Come on, I'll take you up.'

Hazel was just about to go with them, and had even taken a couple of steps towards the stairs, when she suddenly realised that they would most probably want to be alone, and that even the most caring and concerned of mothers could hardly play gooseberry for twenty-four hours a day.

At least Katie had seemed to accept quite happily the fact that she had not put them in the same room.

She couldn't help wondering if Silas himself had accepted this quite as readily.

He was a mature man, long past the stage surely of sneaking kisses, or anything else, behind the back of an ever-watchful parent.

She froze as he came towards her, and then flushed as she realised she was standing between him and the stairs, hastily stepping to one side.

The look he gave her unnerved her. It seemed to see right inside her skull and left her feeling as though he knew far too well just how ambivalent her feelings towards him were.

As she went into the kitchen, determined not to stand there watching them as Katie slid her arm through his and they went up the wide flight of stairs side by side, she acknowledged miserably that the last thing she had anticipated, when she had worried over the problems attendant on this visit, was that she herself might be physically aware of Katie's lover, and in such an intense way that it suddenly felt as though her skin had become a little too tight for her body, as though somehow her flesh had become over-sensitive and slightly sore.

She hated knowing that she was so responsive to Silas. Hated realising that in some awful, dreadful way she was almost jealous of Katie's relationship with him. And yet why should she feel like this? There had been times in the past, it was true, when she had yearned, ached almost if she was honest, for a man of tenderness and concern who would love her, physically and emotionally, but she had quickly learned to put such foolish daydreams from her and to concentrate on reality; those men had never been real, they had merely been vague, fictional characters—a focus for her needs. There had never been a man, a real-life man for whom she had felt the sharply dangerous stab of desire she had felt this afternoon. Perhaps naïvely she had never imagined there could be such a man. She had always imagined that, for her, sexual desire could only follow on from a long-established emotional rapport; and since she never allowed any man to get close enough to her to form that kind of bond she had felt herself safe from the sharp pangs of hunger which now clawed so shockingly at her.

She was standing stock still, staring unseeing into the Yorkshire pudding batter when Katie erupted into the kitchen, exclaiming excitedly, 'Well, Ma, isn't he the most gorgeous man you've ever seen?'

'He seems very pleasant,' Hazel responded colourlessly.

Katie frowned and demanded scornfully, '*Pleasant?* Come on, Ma. He's as sexy as hell and——'

'Katie, I must get the Yorkshires in,' Hazel interrupted her frantically. The last thing she wanted was a blow-by-blow description of Silas's sexual prowess, and not just because she felt he was totally wrong for her daughter. She didn't want to hear it because... Because she was mortally afraid that she simply could not bear to hear it.

'Ma, what's wrong?' Katie was frowning now, the happiness dying out of her voice and her eyes. She came over to the cooker, and removed the full tin of batter from Hazel's hands, firmly putting it down and then turning her mother round to face her.

'You *don't* like him, do you?' she accused.

'No—yes. Of... I... Oh, Katie, I've only just met him, and——'

'Ma, please,' Katie begged urgently. 'Just give it a chance. I know you're going to love him.'

It was an unfortunate choice of verb to say the least, and part of her, a strange, unfamiliar and totally unwanted part, cried out rebelliously, Why should I love him? Because you do? Can't you see how wrong he is for you?

'What is it exactly about him that you don't like?' Katie demanded when she remained silent.

What could she say?

All she could manage was a strangled, 'Well, it isn't that I don't like him, darling; it's just that, well, he's so much older than I'd imagined.'

'Older.' Katie's frown deepened as she demanded almost aggressively, 'What on earth has his age got to do with it? And anyway I think he's just the right age.'

Hazel bit her lip, mangling its already sore swollenness between sharp teeth as despair flooded her. Already it was happening—already he was driving them apart. Of course Katie thought he was the right age and she had been stupid to bring up such a contentious subject.

Desperately she tried to find safer ground, asking as casually as she could, 'You never said how long you intended to stay.'

'Well, *I* can only manage a couple of days, but Silas will be here until Christmas if that's OK with you.'

'Until Christmas!' Hazel gaped at her and discovered that she had to lean against the units for support. 'But Katie, that's impossible. I mean——'

'No, it isn't,' Katie argued stubbornly. 'Why *shouldn't* he stay here? When he told me that he was setting his new book here in Cheshire and that he wanted to do some research in the area, I knew immediately that this would be an ideal base for him. *He* wasn't so sure at first. It took me a while to persuade him that you wouldn't mind.'

Hazel stared at her, unable to utter anything other than a rather numb, 'Really?'

Giving her a sharp look, Katie acknowledged, 'OK, so maybe I should have asked you first, but I know if I'd told you that one of your favourite writers was giving a brief series of lectures to us, and that I'd invited him up here because I knew he was looking for somewhere local to stay while he researched his next book, I knew you'd throw forty fits and raise all manner of objections, but you can't let me down now, Ma, and he won't be any trouble. I doubt if you'll even know he's here,' she added with supreme disregard for the expression on her mother's face.

'I mean, he could have Gramps's old bedroom. That has its own bathroom, and he could work in Gramps's study. He'll probably be out most of the time anyway. He said he wanted to visit Gawsworth, and just think how thrilling it will be when his book comes out, to know that it was actually written here.

'You'll have to pin up a huge notice outside saying, "Charles Kershaw wrote here".'

'Charles Kershaw?' Hazel stared at her. 'But his name's Silas Jardine.'

'Yes, that's his *real* name, but he writes under the name of Charles Kershaw. Kershaw was his mother's maiden name apparently, and Charles is his middle name. He told me that when he first started to write he was still lecturing full-time and that that was why he chose to write under a different name.'

Hazel raised her hand to her forehead in an unconscious gesture of confusion.

Silas was Charles Kershaw, one of her favourite authors, and Katie had invited him to stay here while he researched his latest book. Katie, her daughter, and Charles Kershaw were lovers...

She thought of the subtle and skilled sensuality of the romantic passages in his novels and was shaken by a surge of betraying envy for her daughter, coupled with a shocking conviction that that skill, that subtlety was completely wasted on someone as young as her ebullient, boisterous daughter.

Immediately she clamped down on such destructive thoughts. Thoughts she had no right to allow into her mind. Behind her she could hear Katie saying in bewilderment, 'What's wrong with you? I thought you'd be thrilled...'

Hearing the love and the anxiety in her voice, Hazel forced herself to put aside her own feelings to exclaim wryly, 'Just as you thought I'd be thrilled when you brought all those snails in from the garden and set them free on the kitchen floor.'

'Well, you complained because they were eating your delphiniums and you'd said you didn't want to kill them. Although I do seem to remember you threatening to kill me instead.'

Suddenly they were both giggling, the release from her earlier tension bringing emotional tears to Hazel's eyes.

'Oh, Katie,' she protested helplessly, sniffing them away. 'I can't——'

I can't have your lover staying here, she had been about to say, but just as she spoke Silas himself walked into the kitchen, looking keenly at her and then just as keenly at Katie.

Conscious of her flushed face and tear-wet eyes, Hazel turned back to the oven, quickly opening the door and ladling the batter into the now almost overhot fat.

While it spat its aggression at her, she heard Katie exclaiming brightly and falsely to Silas, 'I've just been revealing your true identity to Ma, Silas, and although she's too overcome with awe to tell you so herself, she's thrilled to bits that you're going to be staying here. She can't wait to boast to all her friends about you, can you, Ma?'

'Katie,' Hazel protested, flushing angrily as she closed the oven door and rounded on her daughter. Perhaps her father had been right after all when he had accused her of being far too lenient and indulgent towards her daughter. Her indignation flashed brilliantly in her eyes as she turned towards Katie, but once again she was forestalled as Silas himself intervened pleasantly.

'I really am grateful to you, Hazel. I must admit when Katie first suggested I base myself here with you while I worked on my new book I was a little dubious. Of course, it was marvellously kind of you to offer to put me up, but writers aren't the easiest of people to live with, especially when they're working, and I was afraid that Katie might have unwittingly painted an over-glamourised version of what having me staying here would be like. But I must say that having met you I realise how uncomplimentary those fears were. It's obvious to me that you are an eminently sensible lady, despite the rather contentious comments to the contrary made by your daughter.'

Hazel gaped at him, blinking in disbelief as she listened to what he was saying.

'Great,' Katie beamed happily. 'I'm glad that that's all settled, although you'll have to move bedrooms, Silas. I was saying to Ma that you'd be much better off using Gramps's old room. It's got its own bathroom for one thing and a huge bed,' Katie informed Silas breezily, turning away before she saw the painful flood of colour that burned her mother's face.

Silas saw it though, and through the tremor that convulsed her, and the tears of shame and self-dislike that stung her eyes, she could feel his steady regard.

Dear God, don't let him guess what she was thinking. Katie was too young, too blind, too selfish as the young *were* selfish, to suspect what she was going through, to guess at the bitter, envious thoughts distorting her mind, to even think in the most fleeting fashion that she, her mother, might feel the most acute despair at the thought of Katie and Silas sharing the old-fashioned double-bed which had been so well designed to accommodate the bodies of two eager lovers.

But her despair was not, as she had first believed, generated by mere concern for her daughter's emotional safety. No; it was generated by a far less palatable and acceptable emotion. It was generated by jealousy.

There, she had admitted it! Made herself confront it. When she pictured Katie and Silas together in bed, she was jealous of her daughter. She was envious of the fact that Silas desired her, that Silas wanted her. What was the matter with her? Did she really want to trade places with Katie? Did she really imagine for a single second that Silas would find *her* in any way attractive or desirable? One only had to compare her with Katie to realise the impossibility of that.

Katie was young, nineteen. She was thirty-six, her body not a girl's any longer, but a woman's.

She had given birth, produced a child. *This* child, who now stood in front of her, a fully formed and very beautiful young woman, poised on the threshold of her most sexually powerful years, while she... while for her those years were over. Her figure was still trim enough, enviably so according to most of her friends, but it was not a girl's body. Her skin did not have the clear bloom of youth that belonged to Katie's... her face did not have the soft youthful plumpness that still clung to Katie's bones. No man in his right mind comparing them could possibly prefer her physically to Katie, especially not a man who had already made it obvious that he preferred the allure of young flesh.

Not even to herself was she prepared to admit that she wished Katie had kept Silas's real identity to herself. She had often wondered about the man who had written the books she had enjoyed so much; now that she was confronted with the reality, she was disappointed. Physically, he might be the most exciting man she had ever seen, but mentally, emotionally... for all the confusion of her unwanted desire for him, she could not help feeling let down by the knowledge that the strength, the maturity, the compassion she had felt so powerfully in his books were all simply an illusion and that he was weak and vain, empty of all the strengths she had envisaged him possessing.

Perhaps it was just as well, she thought tiredly. At least that knowledge should help her to live through the next few months.

'You see, Silas, I was right,' Katie was continuing happily. 'I knew the moment you told me that you wanted a base in Cheshire to do your research from that you'd love it here with Ma. She might not look it but she can be quite a dragon when she needs to be. She'll make sure no one interrupts you.'

Hazel checked her unproductive thoughts and gave her daughter a considering look.

Katie looked so innocent and young, but she was still a woman. Woman enough, perhaps, to try to ensure that no one trespassed into her lover's life when she couldn't be with him by placing her own mother on guard over him. But then who was to guard the guard?

She already knew the answer to that one. She must do it herself; she must make sure that she kept so strict a control on herself that no one, and especially not Silas himself, ever guessed how treacherously aware of him she was.

At least she could be thankful for one thing. He was hardly likely to make a pass at her. Hardly indeed. She might be several years his junior, but she was almost double her own daughter's age.

Stop it. Stop it, she warned herself angrily. What on earth was the matter with her? Normally the last thing she wanted, the last thing she thought about, the last thing that worried her was the knowledge that as an object of male desire she was perhaps past her prime. No, indeed! Since her father's death she had found herself quietly glad that she no longer had to put such a guard on her sexuality, that she was now of an age when men no longer felt compelled to flirt with her.

It was all very well for Katie to complain that she behaved like a middle-aged woman when she was still amazingly young. Katie had never had to contend with the sort of male curiosity that sprang from their knowledge of her past, their awareness of Katie's own illegitimacy and the unflattering conclusions they tended to draw from these facts, and she prayed that she never would.

While not for a moment would she have ever wished that her daughter's life had never begun, she wanted far more for Katie than she had had in her own life. She loved her daughter, adored her, and hoped that Katie too would one day know the joy that came from having a child, but not until she was mature enough to carry the burdens that went with that joy. Not until she was in a position to share that joy and that burden with a man who loved her as she deserved to be loved.

'Oh, by the way, Ma, I forgot to tell you. Gran came up to see me the other week.'

Hazel focused on her daughter.

'Ann ... How is she?'

'Blooming,' Katie told her with a grin. 'And guess what? She's got the most gorgeous boyfriend. Well, man friend I suppose he is really. He's younger than her, at least ten years, but he obviously adores her, and she's over the moon. You should have seen the pair of them holding hands and gazing into one another's eyes ... I felt quite *de trop*.

'They're spending Christmas and the New Year in Switzerland and she's invited us both to go out there for the New Year. She said she'd be in touch with you and sent you her love.' Her face changed suddenly as she added quietly, 'You know, she told me that I look very like my father. She said that sometimes she almost forgets what he did look like and then she sees me and it brings him right back to her. Can you remember him, Ma, I mean physically?'

Physically. Hazel went poppy-red, and then realised abruptly that her daughter was not meaning could she remember Jimmy in any sexual sense but rather was enquiring if she could remember the way he looked.

'Yes and no,' she told her quickly, acutely conscious that for all his silence Silas was watching her very closely. Did he think it was amusing or merely rather pathetic that Katie had been conceived as the result of two naïve children experimenting with sex, rather like playing with a box of matches, with equally disastrous results?

If she knew Katie, he would not have been spared any details of her history. Katie was all sunny openness about her family history, which was her own fault, because she had been determined right from the start that any burdens of guilt that were to be carried for Katie's birth would be carried by her. She had never pretended to Katie that hers and Jimmy's had been the love story of the century. Katie had grown up knowing that her father was dead, and as soon as she was old enough to understand the truth Hazel had gently explained to her how she had been conceived.

She knew that Ann had been equally frank, and was grateful to Jimmy's mother for the support she had given her in ensuring that Katie did not make the mistake of glamourising or idealising her father, but had grown up knowing him almost as a sibling rather than a parent.

The Jimmy she could remember was a teenager, a child almost; the idea of her loving him was totally ludicrous. She mourned the loss of his youth, yes, but if he had lived, if he had not had that fatal accident, she knew that they would now be two strangers with nothing more in common than the child they had brought into the world.

'Do you think if he'd lived you'd have married him?' Katie asked her curiously, unconsciously mirroring her own thoughts.

Instinctively gnawing her bottom lip as she always did in moments of tension, Hazel wished that Katie could be a little less forthright and a little more tactful. It wasn't a subject she wanted to discuss in front of Silas, but then she supposed bleakly that Katie had no secrets from him, and imagined, because of that, that her mother would have none from him either. She had forgotten at times how wonderfully selfish and self-absorbed the young could sometimes be.

Because she had always striven to be honest with Katie, she said, as matter-of-factly as she could, all too conscious of an intense desire to look at Silas, to see how he was reacting to all this, battling with an equally intense reluctance to reveal anything of herself to him, 'I don't honestly know, Katie. I suspect that Dad would probably have put pressure on us to do so, but we were far too young to even think of marriage, and if we had married it would have been a disaster for us and for you. Jimmy was only seventeen.'

'And you were only sixteen. You could have had me adopted.'

'I didn't want to,' Hazel told her firmly. 'And I was lucky that Dad was prepared to stand by me and support me. It was a terrible shock to him, I know.'

'And to you?' Katie suggested. 'I mean, you couldn't have intended to get pregnant . . . but then I suppose the Pill wasn't as freely available in those days and anyway——'

'Er—I'm sure Silas isn't interested in all this, Katie,' Hazel interrupted her, wondering why on earth her daughter had chosen to resurrect this of all subjects.

When Katie herself had been entering womanhood, she had spent many many long hours discussing with her every nuance of her brief relationship with Jimmy... baring her own soul with painful honesty, admitting to her daughter that she had been far too naïve to think beyond the immediacy of what she was doing, that she had not even particularly desired Jimmy or sex, but that she had simply gone along with what he suggested because it was what he wanted. She had loved him, yes, but with the same intense adolescent love she might have given to a best friend or a close relative. There had been nothing remotely sexual in that love; she had been far too immature to experience such emotions and needs.

'Oh, Silas knows all about your lurid past,' Katie told her carelessly, oblivious to her sharply indrawn breath, or the way her eyes darkened with pain. 'He couldn't believe it when I told him how young you are. I think he thought you must have been altering your birth certificate. Well, you see for yourself now, Silas, that I wasn't lying.'

'Yes, I can.'

The terseness in his voice made Hazel glance worriedly at him. Something had obviously upset or annoyed him. He was frowning quite intimidatingly, and she quailed inwardly for Katie's sake, hoping he would not vent his irritation on her vulnerable head. That was the problem with such an unequal relationship—Katie would never, ever be any true match for him and she was positive that he would make sure that the balance of power in their relationship was always weighted in his favour and that Katie always remained the adoring acolyte worshipping at his feet.

And yet there was nothing remotely worshipful in the grin Katie had given him as she too registered his curtness.

'You'll have to watch him, Ma,' she warned Hazel teasingly. 'He's got a terrible temper, frightens us all to death in class.'

Hazel frowned herself. She didn't like the idea of Katie being involved in a relationship with a man who was potentially violent, although Katie herself seemed to have no such reservations.

If she was honest with herself, she did not like the idea of Katie being involved with him at all.

While Katie chattered her way enthusiastically all through supper, describing her new life as a student, Hazel remained almost silent.

She had so looked forward to this, her daughter's first visit home, never imagining she would not come alone.

She put down her knife and fork, her meal virtually untouched, causing Katie to chide her warningly, 'Ma, you don't eat enough. Men like women with a bit of flesh on their bones, don't they, Silas?'

Eyeing her daughter's racehorse-lithe slenderness, Hazel found herself envying her her sleek height and her long elegant bones.

She felt like a dwarf in comparison.

'No sensible man likes to see a woman starving herself into the kind of hungry, bone-thin brittleness that makes her look as though she's permanently hungry. Tastes do vary, of course, but I must admit there is something very appealing to the male ego about the kind of petite fragility your mother embodies... Call it chauvinistic, or old-fashioned—which I suppose in all honesty it is—but such women do in general tend to bring out all the old protective male instincts in full force.'

'But in your books your heroines are almost always positive Valkyries,' Hazel protested without thinking, and then flushed wildly as she realised that she had made the mistake of looking directly into his eyes, and that he was looking back into hers, with the kind of searching scrutiny that made her long to be able to close them and hide herself away from him.

'Not always,' he corrected her. 'Perhaps I've been trying too hard not to betray my own preferences. Certainly I feel it's healthy for me as a writer to take the harder path, to show that vulnerability need not necessarily always come packed in a seven-stone female of under five feet four.

'After supper I wonder if you'd mind if I went straight upstairs and made a few notes? I've had something itching at the back of my mind for the last couple of hours that I'd like to get down on paper, and besides, I'm sure you and Katie have things you want to discuss.

'We haven't mentioned money yet. Naturally I don't expect you to house me at your own expense. Normally when I do this kind of research, I rent somewhere and hole up in it for six months or so, until I've finished my first draft, and I have to admit that when Katie first passed on your invitation for me to stay here I was a little dubious about how it would work. However, you've put all my doubts to flight.'

Hazel had no idea what to say. She had to content herself with giving Katie an accusing look, which her daughter resolutely ignored.

Although this less than loverlike request should have pleased her, for some reason she discovered that once he had excused himself and left her and Katie on their own she actually missed his presence and had to stop herself from listening for the sound of his footsteps on the stairs.

However, now, while she had the opportunity, there were issues she had to take up with her daughter, and she did so as firmly as she could, demanding equably, 'I know I am getting on in years, Katie, but I hadn't realised I was suffering such severe memory loss that I don't have the slightest recollection of having extended this invitation Silas has decided to accept.'

Katie grinned unrepentantly at her.

'Well, I had to stretch the truth a *little*,' she admitted cheerfully, pulling a face as she added, 'Silas can be so punctilious about some things. I suppose it must be his age or something.'

While Hazel was still blinking at this unloverlike comment, Katie continued quickly, 'The moment he told me that he was setting his new book up here in Cheshire and that he needed a base here to work from, I knew it would be a great idea for him to stay here, but I know what you're like.' She pulled another face. 'You'd never have suggested it to him off your own bat——'

She broke off and looked at her mother in surprise as Hazel told her grimly, 'You're right, I most certainly would not have done.'

'There you are, you see,' Katie continued blithely, ignoring Hazel's exasperated frown. 'And I knew that Silas would never agree to come up here without a formal invite so I——'

'Lied to him?' Hazel offered grittily.

Katie's eyes rounded in injured innocence. 'Only sort of. You're going to love having him here, Ma, and I'm going to feel so much happier knowing that you're not on your own. I mean, the house *is* rather remote, and you're here all alone now that I'm away.'

'So it was all done for my benefit, was it?' Hazel asked her acerbically. 'Very altruistic.' It was on the tip of her tongue to suggest to her daughter that while Silas was staying here with her he was—comparatively, at least—safe from other women, and to tell her daughter that she had no intention of acting as a guard dog for her lover, but weakly she knew that she hadn't the heart, and, to do Katie justice, she knew that her daughter *had* been concerned about her living on her own.

'Well, whatever your motives, I don't approve of the way you've manipulated us both. You're not God, Katie. You can't go round interfering in other people's lives. What if I'd denied extending any such invitation?'

'Oh, I knew you wouldn't do that. You're too loyal. Too soft-hearted. But you'll like having him here, Ma. He'll take you out of yourself.'

Hazel stared at her and said crisply, 'Thanks very much.'

In actual fact she doubted if she would see much of Silas at all. She knew from her own experience that when *she* was working the last thing she wanted was constant interruptions—which reminded her, she would have to have a talk with her unexpected guest about mealtimes and so forth. She had just accepted a new commission herself, and, while she was quite prepared to invite Silas to join her for his meals if he wished, she had no intention of pandering to any kind of artistic temperament by providing food and beverages on demand. He must either fit in with her routine or make his own arrangements.

'Just think how well it will go down at the WI,' Katie teased her. 'They'll be asking you to give a talk on what it's like living with a famous author.'

'Hardly,' Hazel told her repressively. 'We've far more important and interesting subjects than that to discuss.' She gave her daughter an austere look. 'By rights I ought to march you upstairs and make you explain to your...to Silas just what you've done.'

'Oh, come on, Ma. You wouldn't do that, would you? He'd be furious with me...'

Furious with her? Hazel gave her a worried look. What kind of lover was it who was furious with his partner? Awful images of violence and oppression flitted through her mind.

'He doesn't...he isn't...he isn't unkind to you in any way, Katie, is he?' she asked cautiously.

Her daughter was, after all, in her own eyes at least an adult, and it wouldn't do to pry too much into her relationship with Silas. And besides, she was too much of a coward to want to be furnished with too many intimate details of what went on between them.

'Unkind?' Katie seemed to consider the question, and then responded thoughtfully, 'No, not really, unless you include giving me the most grotty marks for my last essay.'

Either Katie had totally misunderstood her, or her fears were completely unreal. Fervently hoping that it was the latter, Hazel got up to clear the table and load the dishwasher.

'I'll do that, Ma,' Katie offered.

It was just gone eight o'clock when Silas came back downstairs, and when Katie suggested that the three of them walk down to the village to have a drink in the pub, Hazel quickly made the excuse of having some work to do, feeling that she ought to at least make the attempt to allow the two of them some time alone together. Katie might be quite happy to include her mother in their company, but Hazel doubted that Silas could share her feelings. Although he certainly wasn't betraying any antipathy to her company in his expression, but then he was very good at concealing what he was feeling. Too good, perhaps, Hazel worried as she determinedly refused Katie's cajoling to accompany them.

Modern lovers seemed to lack the kind of intensity she had always imagined must go with being deeply in love, unless of course as established lovers

Katie and Silas no longer felt any urgency to be alone together.

Katie still hadn't said a word about the fact that she had given them seperate rooms, had seemed to accept it quite matter-of-factly. She felt the beginnings of a headache pressing against her temples and lifted her hand to rub the tension away.

'Aren't you feeling well?'

The quiet question surprised her. She turned round to find Silas watching her.

'Just a bit of a headache.'

'You should come with us. The fresh air would do you good.'

'I . . . I'm rather tired. I think I'll have an early night instead.'

Katie had run upstairs to get her coat, and for some reason she felt the sudden burn of tears stinging her eyes. It was all the tension and shock, that was all. That and the fact that she wasn't used to people expressing concern for her, to being made to feel feminine and vulnerable by the concern in a man's voice. She was probably imagining it anyway.

Why on earth should Silas be concerned about her? Yes, she was imagining it, she decided distastefully as she turned away from him. She was turning into one of those silly middle-aged women, so afraid of growing older that she had to fantasise that every male she met was in some way attracted to her. The thought revolted her.

She had been in bed for just over an hour when she heard them return.

As they came upstairs together, they halted on the landing a few feet away from her door.

She tensed indignantly beneath the bedclothes when she heard Silas suggesting quietly to Katie, 'Perhaps you ought to go in and check on your mother, she——'

To her relief, Katie responded immediately, 'Oh, good heavens, no.' But she realised that Katie had obviously misunderstood the reason for his question and had assumed it was concern for her which had prompted it because she went on to advise him, 'Ma hates anyone fussing, especially when she isn't feeling well. Besides, she'll probably be asleep by now. Night, Silas.'

There was a brief silence during which Hazel tried not to imagine them locked in a passionate embrace, but if it had been passionate it had also been extremely short, because she had barely closed her eyes to block out the unwanted vision of their entwined bodies, Silas's arms wrapped firmly round Katie's slender, youthful body, his mouth—that very male mouth with its sharply cut upper lip, and so much fuller, softer lower one, caressing Katie's—when she heard the sound of Silas's door opening and Katie's footsteps disappearing down the landing.

Now she could sleep, she told herself, but of course she did not do so. No—she spent virtually the whole of the night snatching at unrelaxing moments of sleep in between waking up to listen for the betraying sound of creaking floorboards and doors.

What was she doing to herself? she wondered bitterly with tears in her eyes. Of course she wanted to protect Katie, to prevent her from being hurt, but the images dancing feverishly in her brain, the thoughts whirling turbulently through her head, had nothing to do with those emotions.

It seemed inconceivable that she, who had never wanted or imagined herself wanting a lover should so suddenly and so embarrassingly find herself in this confusing and unwanted state of frantic awareness of and yearning for, of all the men, the one who was her daughter's lover.

It was degrading, humiliating...

CHAPTER THREE

OF COURSE, with her having had hardly any sleep at all, it was perhaps understandable that Hazel should have fallen so deeply asleep just before dawn that she had slept right through her normal waking-up time, she realised grumpily, reluctantly opening her eyes.

Someone was knocking on her bedroom door, Katie no doubt, wanting to know why she was still in bed, so she called out, 'Come in'.

She was just lifting her head from the pillow preparatory to getting up when the door opened, only it wasn't Katie who came in—it was Silas.

'Hope I didn't wake you,' he was apologising, 'only I thought you might like a cup of tea.'

Hazel stared at him, completely lost for words. He was dressed in well-worn jeans and a clean shirt, unbuttoned at the throat. His hair was damp and as he came towards her she caught the scent of soap on his skin.

He was carrying a china mug of tea, which he put down on the table beside her bed.

'How's the headache?' he enquired.

Hazel blinked at him. What headache? It was her *heart* that was behaving oddly, not her head. It was beating so erratically, so loudly that she automatically placed her hand over it on top of the bedclothes, trying to steady it.

'Er—it's gone.'

What on earth was happening? She wasn't used to men invading her bedroom, bringing her cups of tea, enquiring about her health . . . especially not men like this one.

She was suddenly mortifyingly aware of the shabbiness of the nightshirt which had originally been Katie's, the untidy tangle of her curls, and the fact that sunshine was streaming through her curtained window and sending far too sharp fingers of light across her bed and her face . . .

She wondered if he had taken Katie a cup of tea, and, if so, if he was now comparing her youthful freshness with the unattractive sight of her own early morning paleness.

'Katie tells me you're an illustrator,' he remarked conversationally, apparently in no hurry to go.

'Er—yes . . . children's books.'

'Are you working on a commission at the moment?'

'I'm just about to start one,' she told him truthfully.

She saw him frown as he exclaimed, 'Won't it be inconvenient for you, having me here?'

Honesty warred with loyalty to Katie and loyalty won.

'Not at all,' she fibbed. 'I'm looking forward to it. I expect they'll ask me to give a talk about it at the WI.'

What on earth was the matter with her? She was behaving like a complete fool.

'Ma.'

She saw Katie coming in through the door with relief.

'Not interrupting anything, am I?' Katie enquired archly as she entered.

Hazel could feel herself flushing, protesting automatically, 'Really, Katie, I——'

'Just teasing, Ma,' Katie assured her. 'Mm—tea in bed. You lucky thing. Why didn't *I* get one?'

'Perhaps because you didn't merit one,' Silas told her drily, causing Hazel to stare at him in confusion. What was he trying to do? Make Katie jealous? Of her own mother? Ridiculous. Of course not . . .

'I . . . I—er—think I'd better get up,' she announced quickly.

'Good idea,' Katie agreed. 'What shall we do today, Ma? I thought Silas might appreciate a guided tour of the area. You know, Gawsworth and that sort of thing.'

'That sounds like a good idea,' Hazel agreed. 'Will you be gone all day or will you come back for lunch?'

Katie was frowning.

'Well, that's up to you. What I meant was, why don't you take Silas to Gawsworth? I mean, it's much more your sort of thing than mine, you know so much more about it, and you know that I'm not that interested in history. Besides, when I was in the off-licence I bumped into Susie, and she's asked me round there today so that we can catch up on all our gossip. You don't mind, do you, Ma? I mean, you love going to Gawsworth, don't you?

You're always saying how much it inspires you and how you never get bored with it.'

Hazel had no idea what to say. Katie was looking appealingly at her, almost willing her to agree. But why? Surely she must want Silas to herself? Unless of course there was something wrong—unless perhaps they had had a quarrel. Perhaps over last night's sleeping arrangements. Maybe Silas had tried to insist that Katie spend the night with him and maybe Katie had felt impelled to refuse because they were under her mother's roof. If that was the case and she was the cause of their quarrel, then perhaps she owed it to her daughter to do what she plainly wished her to do.

Swallowing down her reluctance, she began uncertainly, 'Well, if Mr... if Silas doesn't object to having me as a guide, I'd certainly love the opportunity to revisit Gawsworth.' She had in actual fact been thinking of paying the house a visit anyway.

It was true that she found endless inspiration in its black and white façade, its homely collection of rooms, its history, but she was sure that Silas could have no wish to visit the house in her company. She waited, expecting him to point out to Katie that it was her company he wanted, that he would have plenty of time to undertake his research for his new book once she, Katie, was back at university, but to Hazel's astonishment he turned to her and said with what appeared to be genuine pleasure, 'If you *could* spare the time to come with me, I'd really appreciate it. Katie's told me that you're a very keen local historian, and I suspect I shall be picking your brains on more than one occasion during the next few months. I only hope you don't come to regret your very generous offer to house me.'

'Great, so that's settled. Since I'm not to be offered a cup of tea I'm going to get dressed,' Katie announced cheerfully.

She headed for the door, leaving Silas to get off the bed where he had been sitting.

As he got up his movements dislodged the duvet, which slid sideways exposing, to Hazel's mortification, the upper half of her body in its totally unsuitable covering of a pink and white candy-striped nightshirt embellished with a large picture of a cat. Hardly suitable nightwear for a woman of her mature years, and, while the rest of her body was extremely slender, she was not after all a girl of eighteen and her breasts were far too clearly revealed by the slightly too close-fitting garment.

She made a dive to recover the duvet at the same time as Silas bent down to do the same thing. Their fingers touched briefly, her skin burning as she snatched her hand away, a wild flush of colour dyeing her skin scarlet as Silas looked towards her.

Perhaps he had merely been going to apologise; or perhaps he had not intended to say anything at all, but, whatever his intentions were, they seemed to be forgotten as he tensed, so obviously and so unexpectedly that Hazel automatically turned her head to see what it was that had compelled his attention.

When she realised that it was the soft swell of her own breasts on which his gaze was transfixed, and, even worse, that her nipples, those delicate and normally exceptionally primly behaved indicators of feminine sexual arousal, were flaunting themselves in rigidly taut pinnacles that pushed wantonly against the soft, worn cotton of her nightshirt as though deliberately begging to be touched...kissed.

Hazel couldn't help it. She gave a tiny shudder of self-revulsion and closing her eyes, rolled over on to her stomach and through the muffling thickness of her pillow whispered huskily, 'Please go.'

She was still shivering long after she had heard him leave.

How on earth could she get dressed and go downstairs now, behaving as though nothing out of the ordinary had happened? And what if Silas chose to tell Katie what had happened? She gave a small moan of despair and self-contempt, longing to simply keep her eyes closed and stay where she was, but she couldn't do that. She was a mature woman, not a child, even if she was not behaving as one.

And so she got up, showered in her own small bathroom, and then dressed in a plain black skirt, a cream shirt, and a thick cardigan, which she took great care to fasten all the way down the front, so that even if her body did choose to betray her a second time no one other than herself would be aware of it.

As she scooped the damp towels and her nightshirt up off the bathroom floor, she made herself a promise that first thing on Monday morning she was going to go out and buy herself something to sleep in far more appropriate for her years. Something sensible and middle-aged. Something heavy and thick. Something that wouldn't give away the over-stimulated state of her body, no matter how close to her Silas chose to sit.

Which was stupid, because after what had happened this morning bringing her further early morning cups of tea was the last thing he was likely to do. Nor would she want him to do so. In reality it was all his fault anyway. He had no right to invade the privacy of her bedroom. No right at all. Just because he was Katie's lover, that did not give him the right to walk into her room and perch himself on the end of her bed.

And yet . . . and yet, she acknowledged mournfully, there had been something luxurious, something very special that made her feel pampered and cosseted about being brought tea in bed by a man. Perhaps, she realised with a faint awareness of some deep inner pain, because no man had ever done that for her before. Just as no man had ever held her breasts in his hands, stroking them, caressing their softness, and then kissing them, teasing the erect nipples, until they were trembling with excitement, until *she* was trembling with excitement.

Stop that, she warned herself, frantically, stop it right now. She had no right to have such thoughts. No right at all.

When she got downstairs, she discovered that not only was the table set for breakfast, but that the kitchen was permeated by the delicious smell of freshly filtered coffee. Sniffing it appreciatively, she enthused to Katie, who was just opening a cupboard door, 'You are a love. Thanks for getting breakfast started. I don't know what happened to me this morning. I overslept, I'm afraid.'

She was praying that her daughter wouldn't turn round and see the guilt and the misery in her eyes. Silas belonged to Katie, and she was betraying her own daughter in feeling so aware of him, so aroused by him.

'Don't thank me,' Katie told her, reaching up into the cupboard and removing a packet of her favourite cereal. 'It was Silas's idea. He's a real slave-driver, you have no idea. Said I've been spoilt for long enough, and that it was time someone spoiled you a little bit.'

Hazel couldn't help it. She felt her skin flush and her jaw drop as she listened to this announcement.

What on earth was Silas playing at? He hardly seemed the kind of man who would ever be insecure enough with a woman to need to stoop to those sort of ploys, but then a man of his age, who needed to boost his ego with the company of a much younger girl, must have some serious emotional problems.

And yet in other ways he seemed so mature, so...so in control of himself and those around him.

Perhaps that was it. Perhaps he was one of those men who needed to control the emotions of others and could best do so by preying on the very young. With a woman of her years, for instance, he would never be able to do that. Well, at least not with any other woman of her age, because she would have the experience to match his own, the knowledge, the maturity.

'Er—where is Silas?' she asked Katie, trying to control her rioting thoughts.

'Gone down to the village to buy some papers. He's taken the car though so he shouldn't be very long.'

'Mm…are you making toast?' she asked as Hazel picked up the breadboard and removed a loaf from the bread bin.

'And I wouldn't mind some scrambled eggs if there are any going.'

'Then get up and make yourself some,' a male voice suggested from the kitchen door. 'You've spoiled this brat, you know,' Silas told Hazel, as he walked into the kitchen. 'You sit down,' he instructed her, removing the bread knife from her hand before she could object.

Numbly Hazel did as she was told. What on earth was going on? Silas was treating Katie as though she were a child and not his lover. She knew it was true that she had tended to spoil Katie a little, but her father had tended to be very demanding, especially when he had had his stroke. He had been the old-fashioned kind who took it for granted that a woman should virtually wait hand and foot on a man, and somehow or other Hazel had got into the habit of doing the same thing for Katie, although she had made sure that her daughter did absorb the rudiments of domesticity and taking care of herself.

'I'm sorry, Ma,' Katie said now. 'Silas is right.
You *do* spoil me. Oh, great—home-made bread,'
she enthused as she saw the loaf Silas was slicing.
'Marvellous. One thing I do miss about home is
your cooking. Ma is a wonderful cook, Silas. In
fact she's wonderful, full stop,' Katie added, giving
her a warm hug and dropping a kiss on the top of
her head. 'By the way, Ma, may I borrow your car?
I mean, you won't need it, will you? Not if you're
going out with Silas, and I could really do with it,
if I'm going to see Susie.'

Grimacing at her, Hazel nodded.

'But just see you treat her with the respect she
deserves, and no using all my petrol and leaving me
with an empty tank, and——'

'Put the seat back when you get out,' Katie
chanted in unison with her, adding with a grin, 'Is
it my fault I've got long legs? OK, OK...I hear
what you're saying.'

'You hear it, but will you pay any attention to
it?' Hazel asked her wryly.

'The answer to that question, if she's typical of
her age-group, is no,' Silas supplied as he brought
over a plate of delicious golden brown toast. 'I have
four teenage nephews,' he added surprisingly. 'One
of my sisters has twin boys of eighteen and the other
has one of fifteen and another of nineteen. I
suppose there must have been a time when we were
all equally selfish, but somehow as one gets older
one fails to remember it; hence maturity's la-
mented impatience and exasperation with youth.'

'Just listen to Grandpa there,' Katie teased, adding curiously, 'I didn't know you had nephews. Have you any other family?' she asked him, spreading butter generously on her toast and then licking it off her fingers, for all the world like the little girl she sometimes still was.

'Not really. My parents are dead. I've got the usual assortment of second and third cousins and an aunt or so, but that's all.'

'It's odd that you've never been married,' Katie told him, ignoring Hazel's faint gasp of reproach. Tact, it seemed, wasn't essential to modern relationships.

It was funny that when she had first realised how much older than Katie Silas was it had been her daughter she had been desperately anxious to protect. Then she would have welcomed this albeit unwitting blow to his ego, but now conversely it was Silas's feelings she felt the most need to defend and she had to bite down hard on her bottom lip, still sore and swollen from the previous day's mangling, to prevent herself from objecting to Katie's tactlessness.

'Is it? I suppose I've just never met the right person, at the right time. When I was young I didn't want to settle down; there were too many things I wanted to do with my life first, before I committed myself to a wife and a family, and then later... And then later... Well, I suppose it's true that the older you get the fussier you get, and the more reluctant to settle for anything but the very best.'

A simple statement of fact, or a subtle warning to Katie herself that she must not think in terms of permanency, of commitment, of marriage?

She hated herself for the relief that she felt, and tried to tell herself that it was purely on Katie's account and had no other significance at all.

It was mid-morning before they were all eventually ready to leave. Hazel sighed a little as she saw Katie coming downstairs dressed in a multi-hued jumper, a pair of old jeans which clung lovingly to her long slim legs, leg-warmers which clashed vividly with her jumper and a pair of old trainers, and yet somehow still managing to look stunningly pretty.

At Katie's age she had not had one tenth of the self-confidence of her daughter. What did she mean, at Katie's age? she derided herself inwardly—she didn't have one tenth of Katie's confidence now. Wryly she compared Katie's outfit to her own sensible, sombre-hued clothes.

She looked dull and boring, a plain sparrow standing next to a tropically plumaged bird of far more exotic hue.

Was Silas comparing them as well, mentally berating Katie for deserting him and leaving him to accompany her mother? She writhed inwardly at the thought, half inclined to announce that after all she could not go with him, but good manners, the manners instilled in her by her father and Mrs Meadows, prevented her from doing so.

And if Silas was annoyed by Katie's defection, he was certainly not allowing it to show.

* * *

All the weather signs were that they were going to have an early winter. Certainly, after a dry warm summer, the sudden spate of frosts and cold winds had come as an unwelcome shock at first, but Hazel had always loved autumn. There was something especially invigorating about its cold crisp mornings, its pale blue skies, the pastel colours of its pale sunshine against a landscape washed clean of the warm vibrant colours of summer. Soon the distant hills would be covered in their first falls of snow; soon the last of the leaves would be gone from the trees, leaving them skeletal and bare.

'Brr...it's cold,' Katie complained, shivering as they stepped outside. 'Roll on summer.'

'Summer!' Silas commented, watching as Katie folded herself into Hazel's small car. 'Why is it the young have no appreciation of the truly wonderful things in life? Personally I prefer this time of year, when the landscape is stripped back to its bare bones. It gives it an austerity, a pride almost that you never see in summer.'

His words so closely mirrored her own thoughts that Hazel smiled warmly at him, unaware of how much her sudden pleasure changed her whole face, dispelling the tension and control she was always so careful to maintain and instead revealing a much younger, more vulnerable woman, a woman who in so many ways seemed almost younger and more innocent than her own daughter.

Watching her, Silas wondered if she had deliberately chosen to efface herself, to camouflage herself and hide away behind the barriers she had erected against his sex, or if she had simply fallen into the unconscious habit of doing so.

When Katie had first told him about her home and her mother, in her artless, confiding way, he had been very dubious about accepting her invitation to come and see both of them for himself. Now...

He watched as Katie drove off and then turned to study Hazel. She was watching her car disappear with an expression on her face that was almost wistful.

'You'll have to direct me, I'm afraid,' he told her, opening the car door for her. 'How far is it to Gawsworth?'

'Only about ten or twelve miles.'

Hazel sighed a little as she sank down into the luxury of the car's leather upholstery, wondering a little enviously what it must be like to own such a luxurious marque.

'It's a beautiful car,' she commented, as Silas got in beside her and started the engine.

'Yes. I'm very pleased with it, although they're vastly over-priced. However, when I'm doing the research on a book, I need a car I can rely on and one I can travel in in relative comfort, so something like this is an essential.'

They were almost at the small crossroads where they would have to turn off for Gawsworth, and Hazel directed him accordingly.

'What made you decide to set your new book in Cheshire?' she asked him hesitantly. She had no idea whether he would welcome questions about his work. She had heard that authors could be temperamental over such things, although a show of temperament was somehow the last thing she could associate with Silas. He seemed far too well adjusted, far too quietly self-confident of himself and his goals, but then, as she had reminded herself before, if he was as mature an adult as he had seemed, surely he wouldn't need to support his male ego by choosing such a very young girlfriend as her daughter?

'It all started with one of the characters in my last book, a knight by the name of Hugo de Lupus; a fictional character, related to the Earl of Chester——'

'Yes, I remember him,' Hazel interrupted him enthusiastically. 'He was so well drawn, so interesting, that I found myself wanting to know more about him. And now you're going to base a new book on him? That's wonderful...' She broke off suddenly, conscious of the quizzical look he was giving her, her skin flushing with mortification.

'When Katie told me you read my books, I thought she was flattering me. I see that I was wrong. Yes, I agree with you. I found that Hugo was building into a far more complex and demanding character than I'd ever intended, and, to be quite honest, I hadn't intended to start work on a new book quite so soon. I'd already committed myself to a series of lectures at the university, and I've found that Hugo has rather been getting in the way. Hence the urgency to find somewhere to live while I start my research. I've done quite a bit of reading up on the area; now I need to get down to some proper work. I thought of using a house similar to Gawsworth as Hugo's home base.'

They talked for a few more minutes until Hazel directed him once again and then as though by mutual consent both of them became silent as Hazel settled back in her seat to enjoy the allure of the countryside, and the comfort of the car.

Gawsworth, when they reached it, wasn't busy. The summer visitors were gone, and they almost seemed to have the house and gardens to themselves.

As they walked in silence from room to room, Hazel enjoying the pleasure of seeing familiar objects and rooms, Silas making their acquaintance for the first time, she was visited as she always was whenever she came here by the house's very own special aura.

When they had toured the entire upper floors in almost total silence, she said hesitantly to Silas, 'It isn't a very grand house; perhaps you had something different in mind. We could—— '

'It's perfect,' he told her quietly. 'And you're the perfect companion to enjoy it with. So few people have the gift of silence, of allowing places, things to speak for themselves.'

'Sometimes I think I'm very boring,' Hazel told him shakily, too bemused by his compliment to hide what she was feeling. 'I never seem to know what to say to people. Katie says it's because I'm on my own so much.' She pulled a wry face. 'I don't know so much about that—— '

'You aren't boring at all,' Silas interrupted her firmly. 'The people who are boring are those who chatter endlessly about nothing until they make your eardrums ache.'

They were just about to go downstairs, standing together in the small enclosed space at their head, and, although another couple could have fitted between them with ease, Hazel suddenly felt as though she was standing far, far too close to Silas.

A dangerous sense of expectancy, of excitement, seemed to curl through her veins, gripping her muscles with an unfamiliar tension.

She heard herself saying in a husky, strained voice, 'I think we'd better go down. We've still got the ground floor to see, and then there are the gardens.'

'Yes.'

Was it her imagination or did Silas's voice too seem faintly hoarse?

It was the house, she told herself quickly as they went downstairs. It always brought her a very intense awareness of how many, many generations had lived and loved within its walls, how many, many tears and smiles it must have seen, how many joys and how many tragedies. And it always made her feel vulnerable; aware of her own aloneness, her lack of someone with whom to share her life. Just as, for some reason, Silas himself made her sharply aware of what was missing from her life both emotionally and physically... of all that she had missed.

By choice, as well as by necessity, she reminded herself sharply. There had been moments, opportunities which if taken would have led on to intimacy even if had only been a casual sexual intimacy. But that was not for her. Her body, never having known sexual pleasure or fulfilment, had no craving for it. Something inside her had always made her shrink away from the thought of sex for sex's sake, perhaps because she simply wasn't made that way, or perhaps because of Katie's conception.

But now suddenly she was sharply, almost painfully aware that she *was* a woman; that she could feel desire, that her body could ache and torment her, that she could look at a man, at his mouth, at his hands, and ache almost feverishly to know what they would feel like against her skin.

That on its own was bad enough, dangerous enough, but when that man was her daughter's lover... When that man was, as Katie herself had told her, someone very, very special, then there was no justification for what she was feeling, no pardon for allowing herself to continue to have these feelings, no excuse at all for allowing herself the self-indulgence and the danger of being with him.

If she had any sense, any loyalty, any love for Katie she should have refused outright to accompany Silas this morning.

But she did love Katie. Of course she loved her. And as for her being here with Silas... That had been at Katie's insistence, and, after all what threat did she pose to Katie's happiness? Silas was hardly likely to look at *her* with desire. No matter how much he might have implied this morning that he was enjoying her company, no matter how subtly he might have suggested that he enjoyed being with her, he was in all probability only being polite, being pleasant to her because she was Katie's mother.

Yes, that was what it was: he was simply being pleasant to her for Katie's sake.

CHAPTER FOUR

'THANK you for bringing me to Gawsworth.'

They were outside in the gardens, standing at the top of a steep incline admiring the view of the house, where it lay snugly in a hollow below them.

'I love coming here,' Hazel responded truthfully. 'In the summer they have outdoor seasons of Gilbert and Sullivan, plus a small run of plays, using the floodlit house as a backdrop. People come early to picnic on the grass. There's a wonderful atmosphere.'

'I can imagine.'

Hazel gave him a quick, doubting look, wondering if he was mocking her—if he was comparing her lifestyle to his own and deriding her as a dull middle-aged woman whose life was so lonely and boring that a simple evening's outing became something of immense importance and excitement, far more so than the event actually justified. But when she looked at him there was nothing other than sincere enthusiasm to be read in his eyes. But even so...

'Katie loathes Gilbert and Sullivan. The last time she came with me, she complained that she was eaten alive by mosquitoes.'

'I know the feeling. I experienced the same profound boredom and irritation when I foolishly agreed to accompany my nephews and godson to a pop concert.'

'Katie likes pop music,' she told him defiantly.

'I expect she does. At her age so did I. She'll grow out of it. We all do.'

What did he mean, he expected she did? Surely he must be aware of Katie's tastes, her likes and dislikes? Surely he could hardly have failed to notice Katie's love of the latest pop music, played so loud that it positively hurt one's eardrums? As Katie's lover he must be intimately aware of her likes and dislikes. Or was he the kind of man who had no interest in the woman in his life when they were not together in bed?

Her senses immediately repudiated such a suggestion. Because—or so she told herself—she could not bear to think of Katie, her clever, beautiful Katie being foolish enough, needing enough, to allow herself to become involved with a man, any man, who would treat her so badly.

No, that was more *her* role. She was the one whose inexperience, whose lack of knowledge, whose lack of self-worth, might dangerously lead her into such a relationship. Not that she had the intention of becoming involved in any kind of emotional or sexual relationship, much less one with...

She gave a small shiver. Her thoughts, her feelings, were rapidly escalating and getting beyond her control.

'Cold? That's my fault. I've kept you standing here far too long.'

She was smiling in denial, before she could check the foolish response of her unwary heart, acknowledging that even if she had been cold the warmth of Silas's smile would have dispelled it.

They were standing so close to one another that if either of them took a single step it would bring them close enough for their bodies to brush lightly together, for him to lift his arm and put it around her shoulders, for him to take hold of her and turn her towards him and...

Her stifled gasp made him turn his head and frown at her. For a moment she thought that he had actually looked into her heart and read what she was so desperately trying to conceal.

He was her daughter's lover, she reminded herself despairingly, praying silently for help, for someone or something to help her with the struggle which was rapidly outrunning her self-control.

She tried to concentrate on how humiliating it would be for her, and how painful and upsetting for Katie, if he should guess what was happening to her and tell Katie. Her daughter would have every right to feel shocked and disgusted with her. She felt both those emotions herself and more.

She could not understand why, after all the years since Jimmy's death, when she had never felt the slightest sexual inclination or desire, when no matter how much she might have sometimes ached for emotional closeness with a man who might love and cherish her she had never once experienced anything like the fierce, sharp, painful splintering of sexual chemistry she was feeling now, it had to be for this man of all men.

Was it because he was Katie's... because in some dark and hitherto unplumbed or suspected corners of her psyche, she was jealous or resentful of her daughter? Her soul cringed back from the thought in mute horror. She knew instinctively that it wasn't so. But in that case what was the explanation?

Was it perhaps her age—her hormones? Wild theories and thoughts jumbled together in her head. She had read in magazine articles that sometimes women approaching middle-age were prone to what might be termed erratic behaviour. She was after all thirty-six.

'Does your knowledge of the locale extend to knowing somewhere where we could have lunch?'

The quiet question had to be repeated before its meaning registered. She stared at Silas with panic-blinded eyes that made him frown and search her face, before asking softly, 'What is it? What's wrong?'

She had thought that intimacy between a man and woman began with physical touch, but she had been wrong, Hazel acknowledged sickly as her body, her senses responded violently to the sound of his voice, almost as though its cadences, its warmth, its male tones had thrown an invisible circle around them both, locking them within it.

'I ... I ... Katie will be wondering where we are,' was all she could manage to say.

Her throat felt raw and painful. She was embarrassingly aware that inside she was trembling with shock and emotion. She could never remember feeling like this in all her life. Not even when she had discovered she was pregnant, and certainly not when she and Jimmy...

'I shouldn't think so. She gave me the impression that she intended to spend most of the day with her friend. I may not know a great deal about young women of her age, but it seems to me that once two of them get together they appear to have an endless amount of topics to discuss.'

'I...' Why wasn't she telling him firmly and plainly that she could not have lunch with him? Why wasn't she reminding both herself and him about Katie?

Why was she behaving like such a fool? Just because he was offering to buy her lunch, it did not mean that he wanted...

What? To go to bed with her? Of course he didn't. He was simply being polite. She *was*, after all, Katie's mother, and if he hadn't already guessed the state he reduced her to then her present behaviour, refusing to have lunch with him, and generally behaving like a green girl of sixteen, would pretty soon alert him to the truth.

'I... Lunch would be very pleasant,' she heard herself saying huskily, while her heart bounced around inside her ribcage like a rubber ball, and nothing she could say to herself about good manners and behaving with maturity could truly dismiss the tiny frantic pulse of excitement that refused to respond to all her exhortations to disappear.

They ended up eating at a very pleasant country pub, several miles away from Gawsworth, where they were given a table within a view of the huge log fire, and where the food was simple and very satisfying.

When Silas glanced at his watch and announced regretfully that it was time to leave, Hazel could hardly believe that over two hours had passed so quickly.

He had a way of drawing her out of her normal reserve, of getting her to talk about herself and telling her in turn about himself, that had made her realise how starved she had been of this kind of mental stimulation, how starved she had been of the company of an attractive, interesting man, who seemed to find her equally interesting and attractive.

But that was nonsense, of course. It had to be, she told herself as they left the pub. He was just being polite, that was all. And she, like the fool she was, was over-reacting. The trouble was that she was so unused to male company that she had forgotten how to respond to it.

'Fancy a short stroll before we head back?' Silas asked her, pointing out a footpath that led from the car park. 'I could do with some fresh air, and some exercise to help me digest that lunch.'

Silently, Hazel nodded.

The path led down a narrow lane bounded by overgrown hedges, and then over a stile and across a field, dipping down towards what looked like the course of a small stream.

The stile proved a little difficult for her to navigate. One of its struts was missing, and as she struggled with it she cursed her lack of inches. Someone of Katie's height would have made it with ease and elegance, while she, with her small stature, was having to clamber over it in a most unsophisticated and crab-like fashion.

She had just about made it when Silas realised her predicament and offered, 'Let me give you a hand.'

Before she could protest he was turning back to her, sliding his hands beneath her arms as he leaned forwards and lifted her over the stile so easily that she might have been a child. Despite his age he was quite obviously extremely physically fit, she acknowledged as he lowered her towards the ground.

Although his touch was completely sexless on his part, she was acutely conscious, even through the thickness of her clothes, of the pressure of his palms against the sides of her breasts, and of the intensity and unexpectedness of their reaction to that pressure. And thankful that he could not see what she could feel: that her nipples had hardened and were pushing urgently against the constriction of her clothes as though willing him to become aware of her femininity and its responsiveness to him.

Shame coiled in her stomach and left a bitter aftertaste in her mouth. The moment he set her down, she moved quickly away from him, hoping he would put her heightened colour down to the briskness of the breeze.

Desperate to get herself back to normal, she rushed into nervous questions about his work as she tried to distract her senses away from her physical awareness of him.

He told her that he had always wanted to write, but that as a lecturer he had been well aware of the difficulties in establishing a career for himself as a writer, and had decided that his writing must always be a *hobby* and a self-indulgence when almost by accident he had been introduced to a publisher, through a mutual acquaintance, and had been encouraged to let the former see one of his manuscripts.

'I've been lucky,' he told Hazel, smiling at her when she automatically demurred, for once overcoming her own shyness and hesitancy, to assure him almost fervently that he was one of her favourite authors and that his historical sagas had that special something that made them outstandingly readable.

Suddenly aware that she was perhaps being over-enthusiastic, she stopped abruptly, and said uncomfortably, 'I suppose you must get tired of people telling you that.'

'Never, when it's genuinely meant,' he assured her warmly. 'Although I must admit I do feel rather embarrassed at being the recipient of such undeserved praise.'

'It isn't undeserved,' Hazel insisted, stopping walking to turn and look earnestly at him. 'Katie's probably already told you how much I enjoy your work.'

'She has mentioned it,' he agreed gravely. 'But I rather thought she might be dangling an extra carrot in front of me, so I didn't pay too much attention.'

Not quite understanding what he meant, Hazel hesitated.

'I'm very grateful to you for allowing me to stay with you,' Silas told her quietly. 'A writer isn't the easiest person to have around at the best of times, but most especially when he's working. We do tend to be a rather self-absorbed and selfish lot. I sometimes work quite late into the night. I hope the noise from my typewriter won't disturb you...'

'I'm sure it won't,' Hazel told him. She wondered sensitively if he was subtly warning her that once he was working he would expect to be left strictly alone. Well, she could understand that. Her own work as an illustrator could be mentally and sometimes even emotionally draining, and she too needed her privacy if she was to work successfully.

'I expect you'll want to be left strictly to yourself when you're working,' she said now, determined to make it clear to him that she wasn't going to be forever popping in and out offering him cups of tea and food. 'If you want to make yourself a drink or a snack then please feel free to do so, otherwise—well, I don't bother much with breakfast and when I'm working I tend to have a sandwich or something light, and then in the evening we... I expect you'll want to make your own arrangements.'

'Meaning that that's what you'd prefer me to do?'

His question was too blunt, too direct.

She blinked and wondered furiously what he expected her to say.

'Er...' He was plainly waiting for some sort of response, so she began uncertainly, 'Well, I...'

'You have a very busy social life which precludes us from having dinner together in the evening, much as I would enjoy spending a relaxing hour or two in your company, unwinding from the day's stresses, is that it?'

Was he making fun of her? He must know surely from Katie that her social life was very limited indeed: that she rarely went out, even though her friends were always complaining that she was in danger of turning into a hermit.

Deciding that he must be teasing her, she told him stiffly, 'I was simply trying to say that I wouldn't want you to feel you were under some kind of obligation to eat your meals with me.'

She started to turn away from him, determined to bring what was turning out to be a very dangerous conversation to a close, but as she did so she heard him saying softly, 'Who says it would be an obligation? I was thinking of it more as a pleasure—an indulgence . . .'

Hazel could feel herself starting to tremble inwardly. If she didn't know better she might almost have believed that he meant it—that he was actually subtly flirting with her, that he was actually trying to imply that he found her attractive and desirable. Which of course he could not possibly do.

He was involved with her own daughter, for heaven's sake, and that knowledge, plus her own response to it, was making her feel physically sick.

She prayed desperately that Katie wasn't too deeply in love with him, because she was almost certain he could not reciprocate the intensity of her feelings, and the last thing she wanted was for her precious daughter to be hurt. And sooner or later she *would* be hurt. With a man like this one that was inevitable. Sooner or later there would be someone else, a someone else, who, unlike *her*, would not think twice about responding to his overtures, to his warmth, to his sensuality, and when she did...

She shivered visibly, causing Silas to frown. 'You're cold. Perhaps we'd better go back.'

Go back... If only she could go back to before she had ever met him.

She had known him hardly more than twenty-four hours, and yet those twenty-four hours had changed her life irredeemably. Had changed *her*, showing her facets of her nature, of her innermost emotions and feelings, that she had never known existed. If she had known more about him before she had met him, if she had had time to prepare herself... but she suspected that nothing she could have done could have defended her from the enemy that was within herself.

Her father had been right to insist that she live a life of rigorous celibacy. Had he perhaps in some way seen within her what she had not...?

And yet if for all these years she had had this vulnerability, this aching, welling need for physical contact, for—to put it in its bluntest and cruellest form—sex, then why had it never manifested itself before? Why had she never felt like this with anyone else?

It was a question she was far too confused to know how to answer. Silas had already turned back in the direction they had come and she fell into step beside him, waiting as he mounted the stile ahead of her, and then freezing when instead of crossing it he turned round and held out his arms to her.

As she looked at him, she knew that she had already hesitated too long; that her body was already quivering with excitement and fear that if he picked her up now, no matter how remote and non-sexual his touch might be, there was nothing on earth that would stop her body from responding to him. Even now, standing here looking up at him, between one heartbeat and the next, she could already feel the heat of his body against her own, could already hear the fierce drumming of her own heart, could already sense how her body would melt and yield, silently urging his to respond to its wantonness.

Terrified of what would happen, of how she would humiliate herself and betray Katie if she so much as took one step towards him, she told him raggedly, 'It's all right, I can manage.' She gave him a tight painful smile. 'I am a *woman*, you know, not a child.'

It was the wrong thing to say. The look he gave her slowly encompassed every inch of her, making her feel as though she were slowly melting inside.

'Yes,' he told her gravely, before he turned away from her. 'I do know.'

And as he stepped down the other side of the stile, she was sure she heard him adding acidly under his breath, 'After all, *I* am a man and not a boy.'

But she told herself she was imagining it. That she was letting her own feelings, her own needs put words into his mouth which he most probably had not uttered.

Later she told herself that it was because she was so engrossed in her own thoughts, her own guilt, that, while she managed to negotiate the stile fairly easily, once she was down on solid ground for some unfathomable reason she managed to trip over a totally non-existent bump in the ground.

Her small cry of apprehension was automatic, and so was the speed with which Silas turned round and caught hold of her, dragging her up against his body so that she was locked against him with far more intimacy than she would have been had he merely been helping her over the stile.

This could not be happening, she told herself despairingly as she felt the frantic thud of her heart and breathed in the warm, intimate male scent of him.

The wind had tousled her curls, blowing them across her cheek, and perhaps initially it was simply in automatic response to this that he lifted his hand and gently brushed them back, tucking them behind her ear, while he looked gravely into her eyes as though he was searching for something, waiting.

Later she told herself that this was when she ought to have pushed him away, ought to have made some move to let him know that his intimacy was unwelcome, when she ought to have remembered Katie, but instead she simply stared back at him, her lips parting slightly as she tried to breathe in enough oxygen to satisfy her cramped lungs, her ribcage lifting abruptly as she tried to breathe deeply, flattening her breasts against his body. With both of them wearing so many layers of clothes, it was impossible surely for him to feel their softness, much less be aware of the swollen, aching hardness of her nipples, and yet, she acknowledged painfully, he must have felt something, must have read some kind of invitation in her eyes if not in her body, because the hand resting against her curls suddenly became caressing, his thumb stroking her gently behind her ear, rather as she might have fondled a soft-furred cat, she thought dizzily, trying to fight against the sensations his touch engendered.

She knew she was breathing far too rapidly, that she was foolishly betraying things that should have been kept hidden. Another woman, a more experienced, accomplished woman, would never have reacted so immediately, nor so embarrassingly to so light a caress. Not even a caress really, more a subtle question, a suggestion...something from which both of them could quite easily have withdrawn and dismissed as a mere accidental brushing of his fingers against her skin, if she had not over-reacted so wildly to it, her body trembling, her eyes widening, her breath coming in tiny, frantic little gasps, that were surely as much of an invitation to him as though she had spoken the words out aloud.

Certainly he seemed to have no difficulty in correctly interpreting their message, because before she could even think of fighting, to check what she was feeling, his hand had cupped her jaw, turning her face up towards his. His body had somehow moved subtly closer to hers so that she was intimately aware of its strengths, and its weaknesses, although she tried frantically to deny the knowledge that the pulsing hardness she could feel so intimately had any existence outside her own over-active imagination.

Perhaps if she hadn't been so desperately fighting *that* battle she might have managed to anticipate his kiss and to evade it, but as it was all she could do was to stare helplessly into the depths of his eyes like a mesmerised teenager, knowing that he was going to kiss her, knowing that she should stop him, and at the same time knowing that she was not going to do so.

For twenty years the only kisses she had known had been those of a very shy and reserved father, those of an exuberant and loving daughter, those of friends, brief female pecks on the cheek, and occasionally, very occasionally, when she had not been able to evade or avoid them, the unwanted and unwelcome and totally unarousing kisses of certain of her male acquaintances. Her only memories of Jimmy's kisses were vague and unreal. He had bitten her lip once and it had hurt her. He had also scoffed at her reluctance to indulge in what he had termed 'French kissing' which to her at the time had seemed a distasteful and wholly unappealing activity.

And yet for all her lack of experience, for all her years of celibacy, somewhere hidden deep inside her and unrecognised by herself must have lurked some kind of inner knowledge and instinct, because the moment Silas's lips touched hers, her mouth seemed to swell and soften, her lips clinging eagerly to his, her eyes closing, so that when he almost immediately broke the tormenting contact of his mouth on hers, her eyelids lifted, heavy with arousal and need, her eyes dark with confusion, her lips still parted so that when his returned to caress them again she felt it could only be because her own had begged him to do so.

Three times or maybe four he repeated the light caress, and each time as she reluctantly opened her eyes, convinced that it was over, that he was about to push her away from him and let her go, she was confused by a question she seemed to read in his eyes but was unable to answer.

It was almost as though he was waiting for something, but what?

Her lips felt swollen and sensitive. She touched them with the tip of her tongue exploratively and then tensed as she heard Silas's explosive breath and felt his hand slide from her jaw into her hair, his fingers tangling in her curls.

He said something under his breath. She thought it might have been her name, but she wasn't sure, and then as she looked uncertainly up at him, he bent his head and covered her mouth with his.

This time his kiss was neither brief nor gentle. This time...

It felt as though her heart were literally turning over inside her. It felt as though every single one of her muscles had turned to cotton wool, and her blood to liquid heat. It felt...it felt like nothing she had ever experienced in her life, nor expected to experience, and if Silas had chosen to remove every item of clothing from her body and from his and to lie her down right where they stood, among the cool soft grass and the falling autumn leaves, and to possess her body as no man had possessed it since Jimmy's awkward and youthful taking of it, she would not only have not stopped him, but would have actively and very, very eagerly have helped him to do so.

Fortunately he did not choose to do so. Fortunately he chose instead to lift his mouth from hers, and to press tiny biting kisses along her throat, and even more fortunately when he reached her ear he chose to whisper raggedly into it, 'We shouldn't be doing this.'

They most certainly should not. She froze immediately, sickened and disgusted by her own behaviour, wrenching herself out of his arms so determinedly and so speedily that he automatically let her go.

'No, we shouldn't,' she told him bitterly.

She was shaking so much that he had to be aware of her reactions. How could she have done this...? How could she have allowed it to happen? And why had it happened? He was obviously a man with not just a high sex drive, but a virtually uncontrollable sex drive—he *had* to be, otherwise he would never, ever have attempted to touch her. She was Katie's *mother*, for heaven's sake.

And yet... and yet nothing about him had suggested that he lacked self-control...

But then neither had anything about him suggested that he had the kind of ego and lack of maturity which forced him to bolster himself up by seducing teenage girls. Perhaps that was it. Perhaps his vanity was massaged by the thought of having them both, mother and daughter. Perhaps...

Wild thoughts followed one another like hounds after a fox, out of control and eager to cause destruction.

She was trying desperately to control her emotions, her breathing, the tumultuous beat of her heart and the body that still ached for him so much that she could hardly believe it was *her* body, *her* emotions, that were reacting like this. She felt stupidly close to tears, and tears were something she simply never allowed herself. She had learned years ago the futility, the danger of becoming lachrymose and self-pitying.

Now she felt more vulnerable, more afraid than she could ever remember feeling in her whole life, and all because of this man, she reflected bitterly... all because of this man who had no right to make her feel such things. *This* man who was supposed to be committed to her daughter. *This* man with whom she had just betrayed that commitment and Katie herself.

She couldn't bear the burden of her own guilt. She wanted to demand to know if he had any thought at all for Katie, if he realised what he had done, if he, like her, was suffering any feelings of guilt, of anguish, but she simply could not bring herself to utter her daughter's name. Not so soon after she had been in his arms. She had been responding to him with such abandon, such eagerness. She had been the one to partner him in that betrayal. To mention Katie's name now would be like betraying her daughter a second time.

Instead she had to content herself with a low-voiced, 'How could you? How could you behave so...so vilely?'

As she turned away from him, she saw him frown. 'You're over-reacting a little, aren't you?' he demanded curtly.

She held her breath, tense with bitterness and self-loathing. Another second and he would be telling her, 'It was only a kiss.' Well, she might be inexperienced, but that had not been 'only a kiss', and as for over-reacting...

She gave him a fiercely condemning look and said angrily, 'Over-reacting? I don't think so. Not in the circumstances.'

His frown deepened. 'I see. It seems I totally misread the situation.'

Caution and self-preservation warned her not to respond, but she was being driven by her guilt and her pain and so she ignored caution and demanded icily, 'What do you mean?'

The look he gave her was level and thoughtful. Not the look at all of a man consumed by guilt or ego.

'I think you know what I mean.' He said it almost gently, almost in the manner of an adult to a wayward child.

'No, no, as a matter of fact I don't,' she told him, her voice too high and pitched too sharply.

Still he was regarding her with that gravely questioning look that was beginning to unnerve her so much.

'Very well,' he said slowly. 'I imagined—thought—that what happened between us was not something to which you were, shall we say, averse?'

It took several seconds before his meaning seeped in and, when it did, she saw red.

'You mean it was all *my* fault?' she demanded furiously. '*I* tempted you? I suppose you're the kind of man who'd . . . who'd rape a woman and then claim that it was what she wanted.'

She was too overwrought to know what she was saying, to realise how offensive she was being, until his face changed and he said sharply, 'Now, just a minute . . .' He took a step towards her and when she shrank back, thoroughly frightened of what she saw in his eyes, he seemed to take a deep breath and force back whatever it was he was feeling before saying more calmly, 'I wasn't for one second suggesting that you were to *blame* . . . that either of us was to *blame*. I don't even think it was something that involved an emotion such *as* blame. I was merely trying to say that when I kissed you I thought . . . felt that you weren't averse to what was happening between us, or rather what I *thought* was happening between us.'

His voice had become faintly hard again, and it hardened still further as he told her unequivocally, 'And as for your comment about rape, let me assure you that the thought of forcing a woman, any woman to have sex with me is something I find totally barbarous and revolting. I cannot understand what motivates any man to force himself on a woman who doesn't want him, and, if I've given you a different impression, then I must apologise for it.' His voice had become extremely clipped, the revulsion he was feeling so obvious that Hazel felt a fresh surge of self-dislike rise up inside her.

What she was trying to do was to blame him for something for which she knew she had been at least fifty per cent to blame. She wanted to cry out to him to understand that it was her guilt, her horror at what she had done that had made her react so badly, so childishly, that of course she knew that... That what? That he had been quite right to imply that she had wanted him. Wasn't that after all the simple unvarnished truth?

It might be the truth, but there was nothing simple about it ... nothing at all.

'If it helps to ease your mind, to assure you that I shan't make the same mistake a second time, then please let me give you my word that while I'm living under your roof you will be completely safe from any further... misunderstandings of a similar nature.'

What he was saying was that he wouldn't touch her again, and she ought to be thankful for that, instead of feeling as though a dark cloud had suddenly descended on her. And what did he mean, while he was living under her roof? Surely after what had just happened he must have changed his mind about using her home as a base while he worked in the area?

But it seemed he had not, and she felt too exhausted, too drained, too vulnerable still to challenge him on the subject and to demand that he find somewhere else to live. If she did, who knew what he might say? He might even accuse her of wanting him to leave not so much because she didn't trust him to keep his word, but because she could not trust herself.

They had almost reached the car when she asked him in a stilted voice, 'You won't ... you won't say anything about this to Katie, will you?'

She felt dreadful having to ask him such a question, but she could not bear it if her folly was revealed to her daughter ... if Katie were to turn against her because of it.

The look he gave her was compounded of astonishment and, she was sure, contempt.

'Why on earth should I?' he demanded in a clipped voice.

There was nothing she could say to that. Why indeed? His response had certainly put *her* in her place. He was as good as telling her that what had happened between them—the kiss which had had such an intense effect upon her—meant absolutely nothing at all to him.

She ought to have felt comforted, and reassured, but instead she felt achingly empty, bitterly hurt, and more alone than she could remember feeling at any other time in her whole life.

CHAPTER FIVE

WHITE-FACED, her head pounding with tension and anguish, Hazel wondered how on earth she was going to make it through the evening. Katie wasn't a fool. She must be aware of the grim silence between Silas and herself, even if, please God, she could not realise the cause of it.

They had driven back to the house in that same silence, which had persisted even when Katie had returned full of happy chatter about her own day, and it had gone on through dinner and beyond.

It was not that she was sulking, or in any way trying to punish either herself or Silas, although God knew they both deserved to be punished. It was simply that she could not, dared not speak to him because she was petrified of what she might betray if she did. Just as she was petrified of going to close to him in case her idiotic body did the same thing.

And so she had kept her distance and her silence, responding to those comments he did put to her in monosyllabic words.

Telling herself that it was the least she could do, she announced that she was going to have an early night, ignoring Katie's plaintive comments that she would be leaving first thing in the morning and that she had barely seen her.

She couldn't bring herself to make the obvious comment which was that unless she and Silas had made plans for him to visit Katie at university over the weekends it was going to be quite some time before the two of them were likely to be alone again, and that in the circumstances she would have thought that Katie would have welcomed the opportunity to spend some time in private with him.

She was finding it increasingly difficult to force herself to acknowledge that Katie and Silas were lovers, and no wonder, she reflected bleakly as she prepared for bed.

Just what kind of mother was she, she who had always prided herself on putting Katie's needs first? Was it putting Katie's needs first to allow Silas, Katie's boyfriend, to...to...? To what? To kiss her?

She shuddered sickly. She had never felt more confused or unhappy in her whole life. Why on earth was she reacting to Silas like this? Why on earth had her body chosen to show her that it could feel desire, that it could feel yearning and want, that it could be so sexually responsive, that even now...yes, even now, merely to remember Silas's kiss was to reactivate all the emotions and sensations she had experienced in his arms?

It wasn't as though she was a teenager or even a young woman any more. It wasn't as though... As though what? an inner voice demanded rebelliously—as though she was still a woman? Of course she was.

All right, she admitted painfully. So she *was* still a woman, and a very foolish one at that. But why on earth did she have to want Silas? She knew other men, plenty of them, and she had never reacted to them the way she did to him.

She wandered restlessly round her room, knowing that if she got into bed she would never sleep, and then when she heard someone knock briefly on her bedroom door she tensed, the blood roaring in her ears, her pulses pounding.

Silas! But he couldn't . . . wouldn't . . .

She didn't know whether to be relieved or disappointed when the door opened and Katie came in.

'You OK, Ma?' she asked with some concern. 'You look dreadfully pale.'

'I'm tired, that's all.'

Still watching her, Katie sat down on her bed, stretching luxuriously and then demanding with a grin, 'Well, wasn't I right? Isn't Silas gorgeous?'

Hazel felt as though someone had opened all her veins and her blood was running hotly and painfully out of her body.

'He . . . He . . . seems very pleasant,' was all she could manage, as she turned away so that Katie wouldn't see her face.

'Pleasant!' Katie laughed out loud. 'Ma, how could you? Personally I think he's just about the sexiest man of his age I've ever seen. Of course he's not *my* type. He's far too old, for one thing, and anyway he makes it pretty obvious that he isn't interested in immature students. Very politely and nicely, of course. You should see the way he handles his over-enthusiastic female students. It's a wonder to behold . . .

'Ma, what on earth's wrong?' she asked anxiously as Hazel stifled a shocked sound in her throat and turned a too-white face towards her.

'Katie, what on earth are you saying?' Hazel demanded frantically. 'I mean, it's not as though you have to pretend for my benefit, you know. I guessed immediately what you meant when you described Silas as being very special, although I must admit I had expected him to be younger. I mean, he must be forty...'

'Forty-one, actually,' Katie told her. 'Ma, what on earth *are* you trying to say? You couldn't possibly have thought that Silas and I...that we...' Katie started to laugh. 'But that's absurd. Heavens...I can't imagine what on earth made you think... *Now* I understand what you meant when you made such a big thing of which rooms we were sleeping in. Oh, Ma...' She came over to Hazel and gave her a fond hug. 'Surely the moment you saw Silas you must have realised...? He's old enough to be my father.' She paused and gave Hazel a very searching, thoughtful look.

'*Is* that what you thought? That I'm looking for a father figure?' She shook her head. 'Ma, you've brought me up far too securely for me to have those kind of needs. I don't *need* a father, and when the day comes when I do need and want a lover it will be someone whom I can meet on equal terms— someone with whom I can share, not someone with twenty more years' experience of life than me. Not someone who's going to treat me as a child, a little girl. Oh, Ma...just wait until I tell Silas what you thought...'

Hazel reacted immediately, grabbed hold of Katie's arm and saying huskily, 'Katie! No, please, promise me you won't discuss this with him.' She saw Katie's bewilderment and told her, 'I'd feel such a fool, and so embarrassed...'

'I should just think you would. I don't think from what I know of him that Silas would be too pleased at being condemned as the kind of man who needs to bolster his ego with a teenage lover.'

'No,' Hazel agreed hollowly.

'I still can't imagine why you ever thought that he and I could possibly be lovers in the first place,' Katie was saying as she shook her head, as though still finding it hard to believe her mother's folly.

'You *did* say he was someone very special,' Hazel pointed out defensively.

'Well, yes, but that was because——' Abruptly Katie stopped speaking.

'Because what?' Hazel pressed her.

'Er—because...because he is special, and because...because I know how much you enjoy his books...'

'But you didn't tell *me* who he was,' Hazel pointed out.

'Er—no...I wanted to surprise you.'

'You certainly did that,' she agreed grimly, and then added as a fresh thought struck her, 'But Katie, you know I'd never have agreed to have him staying here if I hadn't thought that it was important to *you*. I mean——'

'What? What difference does it make knowing that he and I aren't lovers?'

All the difference in the world, Hazel wanted to tell her, but she knew she couldn't.

She shivered suddenly, wondering what difference it *might* have made this afternoon if she had known then. But what difference *could* it have made? Better that things had stopped right where they had. She might have behaved like one, but she wasn't a complete fool.

A man of sophistication and experience like Silas could never be really interested in a woman like her. Oh, he might flirt with her, kiss her, even have sex with her if he thought she was willing, but that kind of liaison wasn't for her. She was too vulnerable as it was.

Now that she was over the initial shock of discovering that Katie and Silas were not lovers, the relief she should have felt, the relaxation from tension and self-disgust, were swamped by other new fears and doubts.

She reminded herself that she had often comforted herself in her darkest hours with the thought that nothing ever happened without a purpose... perhaps it had been intentional that she should deceive herself into thinking that Silas was involved with Katie so that she would protect herself from what was undoubtedly a very self-destructive and potentially dangerous attraction to him.

After all, what better barrier could there be between them than that she should believe Silas and Katie *were* lovers? And now that that barrier had been removed she would be a fool to try to ignore the warnings of her own common sense.

It was obvious that a man like Silas, a man who was of his age and experience, of his standing, must have had many women attracted to him over the years. The fact that he was not married must surely tell its own story. Despite the fact that he was intelligent, mature, and good company, there must be within him a reluctance to truly commit himself to a relationship or a person.

But maybe like her he was simply choosy, had simply never found the one person to whom he *wished* to commit himself, a treacherous inner voice whispered tormentingly.

Even if that was the case, it was ridiculous to suppose that she might be that person. That she might have that special something that would cause him to...

To what? To fall in love with her? Now she *was* being ridiculous. And what was more, she was behaving like a fool. What she was feeling for him, what she had experienced this afternoon, was plain old-fashioned lust. It had to be. One simply did not, at thirty-six, fall in love in the space of half a dozen minutes. One met someone, liked them, got to know them and then perhaps...perhaps grew to love and trust them. That was the sensible way to do things.

'Ma, are you sure you're all right?' Katie questioned her worriedly.

'What? Oh, yes...yes, I'm fine.'

'Well, you don't look it,' Katie told her forthrightly. 'Oh, and, while we're on the subject, you've made *me* promise I won't tell Silas what you thought and I'm going to demand a promise from you in return.'

'What?' Hazel looked blindly at her. 'What promise?'

'That you won't go all prim and proper the moment my back's turned and ask Silas to find somewhere else to stay.'

Hazel stared at her. How on earth had Katie guessed what was running through her mind?

'You *were* going to, weren't you?' Katie accused. 'Honestly, Ma, just think how that would make me look. There I am assuring Silas that no, of course my mother won't object, and that she'd love to have him staying here, that it was her idea, her invitation, in fact. And then you go and ask him to leave.'

'But Katie——'

'No. You were happy enough to have him here when you thought that he and I . . . well, when you thought what you did.'

'I thought you wanted him to stay here so that I could keep an eye on him for you,' Hazel admitted helplessly, flushing with mortification when Katie burst out laughing.

She said wickedly, 'Oh, did you? Well, let me tell you something, my naïve, innocent mama . . . If I truly wanted to ensure that a man's eyes didn't stray then you can be sure that I would *not* introduce him to you.'

She saw Hazel's face and laughed again.

'Oh, come on, surely you must have seen how gaga every boy I've ever brought home has gone over you?'

'Katie, that's an outrageous thing to say,' she protested huskily. 'They were *boys*...'

'And Silas is very much a man?' Katie asked her softly. 'You'll be perfectly safe with him, you know. If I thought otherwise... and if it's gossip that's worrying you——'

'Gossip?' Hazel gave her an outraged indignant glare. 'Don't be ridiculous. Who'd want to gossip about me? I *am* thirty-six years old, Katie.'

'Even if you don't even look twenty-six,' Katie agreed teasingly. 'Even if you do have half the males for miles around gazing at you like dogs at a juicy bone.'

'Katie,' Hazel protested, genuinely startled. 'That's not true.'

'Of course it is,' Katie contradicted her cheerfully. 'It's just that *you* don't see it. That you don't *want* to see it. Now, come on, I want that promise, otherwise I go right downstairs now and tell Silas——'

'All right, all right, I promise.'

Perhaps Silas himself would decide to leave now that she had made it so plain to him that she wasn't...that she wouldn't... As she recalled exactly what she *had* said she bit her lip miserably. No wonder he had reacted so angrily to her comments. And thank goodness she had not made any direct reference to his supposed relationship with Katie.

If she had... She swallowed nervously. What had happened this afternoon had been completely out of character for her. She was damn lucky that she *had* believed he was involved with Katie. The last thing, the very last thing she needed in her life right now was a man who would use her sexually and then leave her once he had grown bored with her— a man who...

A man who what? that treacherous inner voice whispered provocatively. A man who aroused and enticed her, a man whose touch, whose kiss promised a type of pleasure, a type of fulfilment she could only dream of knowing. So what if it was only desire he felt for her, so what if that desire could only be impermanent, so what if once his work, his book was finished, he would walk away from her without a second glance? At least she would have lived, really lived... at least she would have touched the stars and known what it truly meant to be a woman.

Dismayed by such treacherous, such wanton thoughts, she forced herself to try and concentrate on what Katie was saying, reluctantly giving her the promise she had demanded.

Silas had given her a promise this afternoon, a promise that he would not attempt to touch her again. Would he keep that promise or...?

She could feel her body going hot, her stomach tensing.

Of course he would keep it. And of course she wanted him to. Didn't she?

Despite the fact that Katie had insisted there was no need for her to do so, Hazel was up at six the following morning to drive her daughter to the nearest station.

'Honestly, Ma, there was no need for you to do this,' Katie protested. 'I don't know if I'll be able to make it home again before Christmas.'

'That's OK,' Hazel assured her, adding drily, 'I'm a big girl now, you know. You don't need to come running home every other weekend to check up on me.'

That made Katie laugh at her and tease, 'Oh, yeah?'

Before she drove off, Hazel looked uncertainly towards the house. There was no light on as yet in the room which Silas was occupying.

After she had kissed Katie goodbye and waved her off, Hazel returned to the house.

Today she would have to make some time to turn out her father's study and bedroom, and to remove some of the junk which had accumulated inside them since her father's death.

She would also have to do some shopping. Since Katie's departure for university she had grown used to buying much smaller amounts of food, but now with Silas ...

That's it, she told herself as she walked reluctantly back into the house. Keep your mind occupied with trivia, with mundane household chores; that way you won't have to think about other things. About Silas himself or what had happened between them.

She made herself a fresh jug of coffee and sat down on a stool, nursing her mug.

It was just as well that she hadn't started her new commission yet. That would give her time to turn out the study and do her shopping. She also had some gardening to catch up on, and with Christmas not so very far away perhaps it was time to start thinking about beginning her Christmas shopping.

Anything...anything at all which she could think of to do to keep her mind and her hands busy.

Half an hour later, when she was standing in the middle of the study carpet rubbing her back where it ached from pushing and tugging at the heavy old desk, so that she could clear out its drawers, she heard the sound of the shower running upstairs.

When they had first moved into the house, her father had had two new bathrooms installed, one in what had originally been a small box-room adjacent to his own bedroom and the other next to her own bedroom and the room which had originally been Katie's nursery.

When Katie had been in her teens, a shower and basin had been installed in her room, and partitioned off to provide her with a minute private bathroom of her own.

Silas was still sleeping in the old nursery where she had originally made up a bed for him, which meant that he was using her bathroom.

It gave her an odd sensation in the pit of her stomach to know that he was there, standing under the shower, his body glistening with soap and water, his dark hair plastered to his scalp. She had never been attracted by the thought of overly hirsute men, but suddenly she had a very vivid and erotic mental image of Silas's body; of a narrow pathway of dark hair arrowing down its centre, across the taut flatness of his belly.

Stop it, she berated herself frantically, stop it at once.

The best way to chase away such dangerous and uncontrollable thoughts was to work so hard that she couldn't indulge in them, and, clinging determinedly to that belief, she started pushing at the heavy desk again, trying to manoeuvre it into the centre of the room, so that Silas could sit behind it and get the benefit of the light and the view from the window, and at the same time enjoy the heat from the open fire.

After her father's death, she had gone through his papers, meticulously keeping those which needed to be kept and transferring them to her own desk, throwing away those that were unnecessary, but keeping in carefully marked files those personal things such as old photographs and letters belonging to her father and which she thought in years to come Katie's children might enjoy having.

The desk had then been pushed back against the wall, and the room filled with an assortment of things, including her father's favourite chair and footstool, and several other odd pieces of furniture.

The chair and stool could stay, she decided, the bookcases lining the one wall were already filled, but the cupboards beneath them were empty and could be used by Silas to store his own papers.

As she struggled with the heavy, old-fashioned partner's desk, she wondered if he used a computer or word processor and, if so, whether there would be room on the desk for it.

It was just as well she had taken down the curtains in the spring and had them cleaned. She would have to bring them down from upstairs and rehang them, and . . .

She had almost got the desk where she wanted it; one final push, that was all it needed, but the wretched thing refused to move, and she ended up banging her hip bone quite painfully on it as she leaned her full weight against it.

The pain made her cry out in irritation and frustration. She had realised that the shower had stopped running, but she hadn't realised that Silas had come downstairs until he opened the door and demanded tersely, 'Hazel, what's wrong? I heard you cry out. Are you all right?'

Hot and flushed, self-consciously aware of how dreadful she must look with her curls all tangled, and her top clinging stickily to her skin, her jeans dusty, and her face free of make-up, Hazel swung round to face him. 'I'm fine,' she told him shortly. 'I didn't realise you were down. I'll just get cleaned up and then I'll come and make your breakfast.'

'I'm not a child, you know,' Silas returned coolly. 'There's no need for you to wait on me. I'm perfectly capable of making myself a cup of coffee and eating some cereal. What exactly are you doing in here?'

'Isn't it obvious?' Hazel asked him tartly. Her arms were beginning to ache, warning her that she had probably overdone things in her attempt to move the desk. 'I want to get this room straight so that you can work in here, but this damned desk . . .'

Silas frowned as he came further into the room. '*You've* been trying to move *this*?' he demanded shortly. 'My God, woman, are you crazy? Don't you realise how easily you could have injured yourself?' he asked her grittily without waiting for a response. 'Why on earth didn't you wait until I——?'

Normally equable and even-tempered, Hazel felt all the confusion, the anguish, the pain of the last few days boil up inside her, until ignited by irritation and misery it exploded.

'Until what? Until you, Mr Macho Male, could move it for me?' she demanded aggressively. 'Well, let me tell you something, I don't need your help. In fact, I don't need anything from you at all. I'm perfectly capable of managing by myself.'

Abruptly she realised what she was saying and stopped. Her heart was beating far too fast; she was over-reacting out of all proportion to his comment. She felt torn between bursting into tears and screaming. She hardly recognised herself or her reactions and, although she was unaware of it, some of her confusion and despair showed in her shadowed, stormy eyes.

'Yes, very capable,' Silas agreed drily, so drily in fact that her temper subsided and she looked directly at him.

If she hadn't known better, she might almost have believed that was a touch of wry self-mockery she could hear in his voice.

As though... As though what? As though he was actually acknowledging that her independence, her desire to be self-reliant, rubbed against a streak of male protectiveness within himself which he had not hitherto recognised.

Ridiculous. She must be imagining things, she told herself sternly.

'Actually what I was going to suggest was that the *two* of us might have a better chance of shifting it without injury than one of us alone.'

She had the grace to flush a little, but she couldn't bring herself to offer any kind of verbal apology. She still felt too raw, too vulnerable, too aware of how close she had come yesterday to making an utter fool of herself. She couldn't bear to think what might have happened if she had actually accused him of being unfaithful to Katie. Would he have been amused, or annoyed? She suspected that it would have been the latter. He was far too intelligent not to be aware of the opinion of him she had drawn in believing he was romantically involved with Katie, and she doubted that he would have been flattered by it.

'I'm not sure if this room will be suitable——' she began to say uncertainly, frowning as she mentally checked the number of power points and the size of the desk, worrying about how he would fit in any electronic equipment he might need to use.

The look he gave her was singularly cynical.

'In my time, I've worked quite successfully in a space less than a quarter the size of this. In fact this is sheer luxury. One of the reasons I've sold my London flat and decided to move out into the country somewhere is the lack of space. My rooms at the university are adequate, but barely.

'Fortunately, I'm not a collector of material possessions, or at least I haven't been up until now. When I began my career, I worked, lived and slept in a room in my sister's house which she and her husband generously provided rent free. When I first moved into my flat, although I had thought that I'd enjoy its privacy and solitude, I found that for months I was constantly listening for the sound of feet on the stairs, for the kids' voices. I missed their company more than I'd ever realised I would.'

Katie frowned at him. Why was he confiding in her like this? What was he trying to tell her? That he was a man who hadn't put down roots? Well, she knew that already, but she had assumed that that was from choice. Now...

Pushing her hair back off her face, she asked him curiously, 'If you feel like that, then why——?'

'Have I never married?'

Her eyes registered her shock. What she had been going to ask him had been why he had not moved closer to his family, but he had not allowed her to complete her question and had obviously totally misunderstood it. She would never have dreamed of asking him something so personal.

'Initially because I was simply too busy, and too poor, and then latterly... Well, I suppose it's true that the older you get, the fussier you become. Sexual desire, sexual chemistry, call it what you will, is no longer enough. You want more...much more. You want someone who will be a true partner in all the meanings of the word. Both my sisters are extremely happily married and very much in love with their husbands. I envy them those relationships, and I certainly wouldn't settle for anything less. They've been lucky, and they've worked hard at their marriages. But what about you? A young woman on your own with a small child to bring up—there must have been times when you've been tempted to marry, if only to provide Katie with a father.'

He had been too open with her for her to be tempted to lie.

'Yes, there have,' she agreed honestly. 'Although in my case... Well, Katie had her grandfather. He was a wonderful man, but very old-fashioned. After what happened with Katie's father...' She bit her lip, unable to go on, alarmed by how much she had already told him.

'Yes?' Silas prompted gently, watching her.

'Er—well...' She paused and thought frantically of something she could offer him to silence his questions, and then abruptly changed her mind. Why not simply tell him the truth? Once he realised how very far removed from his league she was in terms of experience, if he had been tempted to break the promise he had given her yesterday then he would surely change his mind.

'Although he never said so, I think my father was concerned that...that history might repeat itself.'

When he frowned, obviously not understanding, she gritted her teeth and told him despairingly, 'He accepted that what happened with Katie was...was an accident, but you see he *was* very old-fashioned, very...very shocked by what I had done, and I think he felt that...that it might happen again. That I might...'

'That you might what?'

'Have another child,' Hazel told him huskily. 'That I might make the same mistake I had made with Jimmy, and become pregnant without being married.'

There was a long pause and then Silas said incredulously, 'But as I understand it you were barely sixteen when Katie was conceived, and her father hardly a year older. You were children, both of you, and it's a credit to your maturity, to your spirit that you've coped so successfully with a situation like that.'

'I had help. My father was wonderful. He supported us both financially. Gave us a home.'

'And forced you to live like a nun?' Silas asked her grimly.

Hazel chewed her lip defensively.

'He thought he was doing the best thing for all of us. And I can see his point of view...'

And you never, never once, wanted to break out of the strait-jacket he locked you in? You never once wanted to——?'

'To what?' Hazel demanded harshly, her sensitivities bruised by the anger she could hear in his voice. 'To have some sort of wild sexual fling? No. I never wanted to do that. I'd better go and get your breakfast,' she added shortly, changing the subject. 'I have to go shopping later this morning, once I've got this room sorted out. Will you be using a computer or a word processor?'

'Yes. But you can leave me to sort all that out. I do know how to use a duster and a vacuum cleaner, you know.'

As she made to walk past him, it seemed as though he was going to reach out and stop her, but when she froze and stared at him he said simply, 'There's no need for you to put yourself out on my account, you know.'

'No need at all,' she agreed curtly. 'Which is why I don't intend to do so.'

She was angry with him and punishing him because of her own folly, because somehow or other he had drawn her out to such an extent that she had confided in him, telling him things she had never ever told anyone else.

She ought to be punishing *herself* and not him, she recognised as she headed for the kitchen. It wasn't *his* fault that she seemed to find him so...so easy to talk to, so...so easy to confide in.

And what on earth he must think of her idiotic admission that she had lived a completely celibate life since Katie's conception she had no idea. He probably pitied her, thinking she was virtually devoid of any kind of normal sex drive. He was probably thanking his lucky stars that he had found out the truth about her before it was too late. She had no doubt that he would most definitely keep his promise to her now.

So why, as she prepared another fresh jug of coffee, did she feel more like bursting into tears than being relieved?

CHAPTER SIX

'GOOD heavens, you've been busy, haven't you?'

Hazel gritted her teeth inwardly, and smiled mechanically as Sheila Simpson stared curiously at her loaded shopping trolley.

Of all the people for her to bump into in the supermarket, Sheila was the very last one she would have chosen. Sheila was the local gossip and busybody, an angular woman of forty-odd who ruled her own apparently perfect family and husband with a rod of iron, and who continually and loudly disparaged those who could not match her own exacting standards.

Hazel had always been aware that Sheila was deeply suspicious of her, both because of her single state and apparently because she considered that Hazel looked far too young to have a daughter of Katie's age.

'Expecting visitors, are you?' she questioned now with false friendliness, her glance fixed on the contents of Hazel's well-filled trolley.

'Not exactly,' Hazel told her coolly.

'Oh, doing a bit of early shopping for Christmas, then, I expect,' Sheila hazarded. 'Of course you'll have Katherine home, won't you?'

It was one of Sheila's many affectations that, as she piously informed everyone, she refused to shorten people's names to some corrupt derivative of the original, and Hazel had never bothered to inform her that Katie had in fact been christened exactly that. Her full name was Katie Georgina, the Georgina being for Jimmy, whose second name had been George.

Without vouchsafing her a yes or a no, Hazel determinedly pushed her trolley past her. It was ridiculous that she should feel guilty for withholding the truth from Sheila, and even more ridiculous that she should feel uncomfortably aware of how avidly curious the other woman would have been had she told her the truth.

She was thirty-six years old, for heaven's sake, and if she chose to invite a member of the opposite sex to lodge with her for a short space of time that was no one's business other than her own.

Besides she could just imagine how Sheila would embellish and extend the truth, how she would serve it up to others, dressing it up with a sauce of sexual innuendo while virulently protesting that of course she knew there was nothing in it and that the relationship was totally innocent.

Hazel had heard Sheila in action before. She specialised in stirring up trouble.

But what did it matter if people did gossip about her? she asked herself later as she drove home. Her father was dead and could no longer be hurt by that sort of thing. Katie was far too modern and youthful in her outlook to do anything more than laugh her head off at the suggestion that her mother was involved in a sexual liaison with someone, and, as for her own feelings, she was of course concerned what her friends, her real friends, thought of her, but they knew her far too well to judge her on Sheila's gossip, and besides she had been urged more than once by all of them to stop hiding herself away, to go out and enjoy herself, to, as one of them had very bluntly put it, 'Go out and find yourself a man, and use what nature has so generously endowed you with before it's too late.'

And after all, who knew? Perhaps they were right and she was wrong. Perhaps she had lived with her father for so long that she had unconsciously adopted his views as her own.

Several of her unmarried and divorced friends cheerfully and frankly admitted to brief affairs, and even in some cases to the odd one-night stand, and evidently felt no shame or embarrassment in doing so, and after all why should they? They were, much as she was, accountable only to themselves. Her lifestyle was an unusual one for a healthy woman of her age. Perhaps if she'd been older when Katie was conceived, perhaps if her experience of sex with Jimmy had been different, she might not have found it quite so easy to fall in with her father's wishes, to suppress her own desires almost before they were born, to relentlessly control every impulse towards expressing her sexuality which she had experienced, so much so that it was now almost second nature, rather like being taught to sit up straight or hold your tummy in—it had become something she did without even having to think about doing it any longer.

Or at least she had. Perhaps in the years since her father's death she had not kept such a careful guard on herself, because she had foolishly begun to believe that at her age she was past suffering the pangs of need and loneliness which had beset her in her twenties, or perhaps she had simply grown careless. She had no idea which of these weaknesses had been responsible for her reaction to Silas.

When she got home, the Jaguar was no longer parked outside. She stared at the space where it had been, her heart thumping. Had Silas perhaps changed his mind and left, without telling her? What if he had gone? Wouldn't that be for the best?

All the time she was walking up the path and unlocking the back door, she was telling herself that it would be a relief if he had gone—that it was the most sensible thing he could do, that she wouldn't be in the least bit upset . . . and yet when she opened the kitchen door and saw the note he had left on the table, she reached for it with trembling hands, scanning it quickly while her mouth went dry and her stomach heaved.

'Gone to Chester to see if I can borrow some research material from their library,' the note read.

She pulled out a chair and sat down in it. She felt weak and oddly light-headed, and she told herself that what she was experiencing could not be relief. Of course it couldn't be, and yet all the time she was unpacking and putting away her shopping, she was listening for the sound of his car, for his footsteps, for his voice.

When she had finished and he still hadn't returned, she paced restlessly around the kitchen, unable to settle to anything.

'For heaven's sake,' she muttered out loud to herself impatiently. 'You're a woman of thirty-six and you're behaving like a girl of sixteen. Anyone would think you'd fallen in love with the man.'

She froze where she stood, suddenly shivering.

What a ridiculous notion. Of course she hadn't fallen in love with him. She was far too old for that sort of thing. Far, far too sensible. Women of her age did not fall in love. After all, she barely knew Silas.

And yet already she had told him far more about herself than she had told some of her closest friends.

That knowledge was like touching the nerve in an aching tooth: highly painful and highly addictive, something to which her thoughts kept returning again and again no matter how much she tried to distract him.

'You know what you're doing, don't you?' she derided herself. 'You're virtually willing yourself to be in love with him. Stupid woman.'

She went into the study determined to banish such thoughts with some physical work, but when she had opened the door and walked inside the room she stood and blinked in amazement.

Every surface was clean and polished, the window sparkled, and the carpet was immaculate. All those items she had put to one side to be disposed of were neatly stacked in one corner of the room, a fire had been laid in the grate and the old brass coal bucket had been polished within an inch of its life.

All that the room now lacked was its curtains, and on the desk stood a modern computer screen and keyboard, neither of them somehow or other looking at all out of place with the heavy old-fashioned furniture.

Silas certainly hadn't exaggerated when he'd said he was perfectly capable of wielding a vacuum cleaner and a duster, and yet for some reason, instead of feeling relieved that she no longer had to face the task of cleaning out the room, she felt faintly aggrieved. Resentful almost, as though in cleaning the room himself he had somehow in a subtle and non-verbal way been telling her that he had no need of her help, that he was entirely self-reliant, that there was no place for her in his life.

But she didn't want a place in his life. She didn't want to become involved in any way at all with a man who, while he might give her some brief passing sexual pleasure, could never satisfy her deeper and more important emotional needs, could never give her the companionship, the emotional stability, the love she had always denied to herself that she wanted, but which in actual fact...

Stop this right there, she warned herself shakily. Such thoughts could only lead in one direction. Such thoughts could only lead her into pain and the kind of heart-searching which would achieve nothing.

She was content with her life as it was. Well, she was reasonably content... as content as a woman of her age had any right to expect to be. When she looked around, how many of her friends, of the women she knew, were truly and happily fulfilled by their marriages in the way they had anticipated when they entered into them? Not many of them, and, while sometimes she envied them their husbands, more often than not she found herself listening to their complaints, their frustrations, and thinking that perhaps after all she was more fortunate than they.

The kind of relationship she had once dreamed so yearningly of was pure fiction, did not exist...could not exist. No single other human being could ever match one's own emotional needs exactly and immediately, and only a fool thought that it was possible for them to do so.

But she did have friends who were happy, who were content, who cheerfully admitted that, while their marriages had matured into far different relationships from those they had initially envisaged, these relationships were good ones; their husbands were men whom they actually liked as well as loved, despite their differences and their disappointments.

She turned blindly towards the window. Was she really content to spend the rest of her life alone? Katie had her own life to live and she had no wish to chain her daughter to her even if that were possible.

So what alternatives were left to her? A steady, secure relationship with one of the men she already knew; there were two or three among her acquaintances who had made it clear that they would like more from her than mere friendship, and who were free and willing to commit themselves to her.

She moved restlessly around the room. The trouble was that, much as she liked each of these men, she did not desire them...did not want the kind of intimacy with them that came with marriage.

So what else was there? An affair... A series of affairs... No, that had never appealed to her. Although she listened with curiosity and sometimes disbelief to her more sophisticated friends' descriptions of their own relationships, the more she heard, the more she herself felt repressed by her lack of knowledge, her own awareness that while she might in terms of years be a woman of maturity, in terms of experience she was as ignorant as the teenager she had been at sixteen.

No amount of listening to other people's experiences could make up for the lack of one's own. Any man who wanted to take her to bed would quite naturally assume that she had the knowledge and the skill to take full responsibility for her own pleasure and a good measure of his. Men, especially older men, her friends told her, were often selfish lovers, expecting, as one of her more frank friends had cheerfully told her, 'That you're going to do all the really hard work and they're going to enjoy the results of it. Give me a younger man every time! They might not have the experience but they more than make up for that with their enthusiasm.'

Hazel did not know why but she did not feel inclined to become involved with a younger man. Perhaps she simply did not have the self-confidence.

No. What she wanted...

What she wanted was Silas.

The thought slid serpent-like into her mind, making her shiver and cross her arms repressively around her body, as though somehow by doing so she could subdue the ache inside her, the knowledge that she only had to think of Silas, to close her eyes and remember what it had felt like when he kissed her, and immediately she wanted him, ached for him.

This was not love. It was lust, she told herself defiantly, and probably the very best thing for her to do would be for her to go to bed with the man and get the whole thing out of her system.

Go to bed with him. She started to shiver, trembling inside with the force of what she was feeling, acknowledging the dangerous insidiousness of her own thoughts, at the same time as she tried to reassure herself that of course she would not want to do any such thing.

Casual sex was not for her. She was adamantly sure of that. And besides... Silas probably didn't want her any more. If her behaviour yesterday had not put him off her completely, then surely her idiotic confidences this morning, which had laid bare for him the paucity of her sexual history, must have done so?

Yes, she was safe enough from any subtle sexual pressure from Silas.

But was she safe from herself, she wondered, or was her self-control finally cracking up?

If so... She took a deep breath; if so then she would just have to keep as much distance between Silas and herself as possible, starting right now.

She might not need to do any work on the study, but there was still her father's bedroom to turn out; the bed to be made up, the bathroom to be stocked with towels.

Silas could move in there tonight, where he would have the privacy of being virtually at the opposite end of the house from her, where he would have his own bathroom. Where she need not go into the house's main bathroom and discover that the scent of his cologne still hung elusively on the air... Where she need not be tormented by erotic images of his body, nude and supple, and so very, very male.

Stop it, she urged herself as she headed for the stairs. For goodness' sake stop it.

At half-past six, just when she had decided that Silas had taken her repudiation of him so much to heart that he was not going to return until after supper, she heard the sound of his car coming down the drive.

She hadn't changed from the jeans and top she had been wearing earlier, and although she was wearing make-up it was no more than she would normally have worn. There was after all no reason why she should make any special effort to make herself look attractive for Silas. No reason at all, and yet before going downstairs she stared at herself critically in her bedroom mirror and decided depressingly that she was perfectly safe from Silas because no man with any sense of taste could possibly find anything remotely attractive in a five-foot-two female dressed in old jeans and a bulky sweatshirt, who wore her hair in a cloud of untidy curls. What she failed to see what was immediately obvious to others, and that was the clear naturalness of her skin, the youthful contours of her face and body, the soft silkiness of her abhorred curls, and the sexual appeal of her slender body clad in its oversized top and snug-fitting jeans.

No, there was most definitely nothing about her appearance which would lead Silas to imagine that she had changed her mind, she decided firmly before heading downstairs.

He was already in the kitchen when she walked in, looking across the room towards her with an expression in his eyes she could not decipher.

She decided that it was probably amusement and was therefore unable to hide her astonishment when he remarked softly, 'You know, I'd forgotten how good it was to have someone to come home to. You do, when you live alone.' He paused and then before she could pull herself together and say anything, he added thoughtfully, 'You must miss your father, and Katie.'

Was he suggesting that he felt sorry for her? A woman on her own?

She looked defensively at him and, seeing neither pity nor mockery in his eyes, allowed herself to admit huskily, 'Yes, as a matter of fact I do.'

'You're still young enough to marry. To have more children...'

Hazel's jaw dropped.

'I'm thirty-six,' she protested, unable to hide her surprise.

'So what? There are women today of forty who are having their first child; women who have spent their twenties and thirties concentrating on their careers, and who have realised that those careers aren't enough, that they want a family as well. Or is it that you don't want any more children? I can understand why you might not feel you want to take on a husband,' he told her whimsically, 'but children...'

Children... She'd never even thought about it. At least...well, yes, she had thought about it when Katie was younger, not wanting her to grow up alone as she had done, but then once Katie had reached her teens...and now... Well, she was thinking more in terms of the grandchildren Katie would one day provide her with, not babies of her own, and yet, as Silas had remarked, there were women older than her who were giving birth and bringing up young families.

'I...I haven't really thought about it,' she fibbed, turning her back on him. 'I certainly don't feel any need to fulfil myself by conceiving a second child to bring up without its father,' she added quietly. 'With Katie I was lucky. She's never reproached me because she's had to grow up without knowing Jimmy. Jimmy's family have always made her welcome as a part of them.'

'Did you love him very much?'

The question startled her. It was one she wasn't used to hearing. Jimmy was so very far away from her now in her past that she found it hard sometimes to remember exactly what she had felt towards him, but she knew it had not been the love of a woman for a man. How could it have been, when they had only been children?

'He was my friend,' she answered honestly. 'I was a very intense teenager, perhaps because I was very lonely. Jimmy...Jimmy was very special to me as a person. But no, I didn't love him as...as a lover.'

She had said far more than she had intended to say, revealed far more than she should have done, and as she swung round and saw the compassion darkening his eyes she bit her lip in vexation, saying abruptly, 'It was all a very long time ago, and hardly matters now. I've cleared out Dad's room for you. It has its own bathroom. I haven't made anything for supper. I wasn't sure if you'd be coming back.'

All the time she spoke, gabbled almost, she was aware of Silas watching her, studying her—as well he might, she reflected dismally. No doubt, as far as he was concerned, she was an odd and rare species, a woman whose one experience of sex had led to the conception of a child, and who had never allowed herself to become a fully functioning sexual woman. Oh, yes, he might well regard her with that thoughtful considering gaze that made her feel so uncomfortable and so...so vulnerable.

'I thought we might have supper out. I'm having a small problem with my work, in that my research has revealed such a wealth of information and detail that I'm undecided as to whether I should only deal with a shorter space of Hugo's life in this book, and then continue it in another. I need someone to listen while I talk myself through the problem, and I wonder, rather selfishly I know, if in return for supper you might be prepared to lend a sympathetic ear.'

'*Me!* But I can't advise you. I don't know the first thing about writing a book. Surely your publishers...?'

'A second opinion is always of value, even if it only helps to clarify your own thoughts. Besides, you said you'd like to read more about Hugo. You already know the character, so don't underestimate the value of your opinion. Don't put yourself down so much,' he added coolly. 'If you aren't prepared to value yourself as you should, then at least don't deny others the opportunity to do so.'

Hazel was too stunned to speak.

'I haven't booked anywhere,' Silas continued. 'I wasn't sure whether you'd be free, or if you'd be willing to help me out.'

When he put it like that, how could she refuse him, or pretend that she was already engaged elsewhere?

'I'll have to change,' she told him uncertainly.

'That's OK—so will I. Is there anywhere in particular where you'd like to eat?'

'There's an Italian place in Knutsford,' she told him. 'I don't know if you like Italian food.'

'I do,' he assured her. 'Do you know the name? I could telephone and book a table.'

Feeling rather as though her life had suddenly escaped from her own control, she gave him the name, and then headed for the stairs.

Half an hour later, standing in front of the mirror and frowning at her reflection in a red jersey wool dress which Katie had insisted on her buying the previous winter, and which was one of the few really smart things in her wardrobe, she wondered what on earth she was doing.

Silas had made it plain enough why he wanted her company, and she did not for one moment doubt that he had spoken the truth, but what about her—what about her motives? Was she honestly and completely sure that she had managed to root out of her system the perverse and extremely disruptive thoughts which had been attacking her ever since she had set eyes on him?

Yes, of course she had! Of course she had.

The restaurant was a small comfortable place run by a large and garrulous Italian family, who recognised Hazel the moment she and Silas walked in through the door, despite the fact that she had only eaten there on a handful of occasions.

The proprietor, genial, rotund, and very, very Italian, came forward to greet them and then exclaimed lavishly, 'Ah, at last we see the husband of the so beautiful lady who dines here only with her friends. I say to my own wife then, that this lady, she is too beautiful to be on her own. All my male customers, they are distracted from their food by her beauty.'

Hazel could feel herself going scarlet, but as she opened her mouth to correct his misapprehension Silas touched her lightly on her shoulder.

When she turned round he shook his head and murmured so that only she could hear, 'I shouldn't bother if I were you, it will probably only lead to further confusion. Unless of course you wish to take issue with him on the subject of his chauvinism and point out that no woman these days needs a man to make her life complete.'

Hazel shook her head numbly, following the beaming Italian to a small table set in an alcove, and romantically illuminated by the discreet lighting and the candles on the table.

'I can't imagine why he thought we were married,' she told Silas uncomfortably when they had given their order. 'I'm not even wearing a wedding ring.'

'I shouldn't let it worry you,' Silas responded, frowning a little as someone coming towards them caught his eye.

Hazel turned her head to see what had caused his frown.

A man in his mid-fifties, accompanied by a girl who could not have been much older than Katie, were being shown to a table several feet away from their own, and it was immediately obvious that their relationship was not one of father and daughter.

'Now, that's something I always dislike to see,' Silas commented quietly to her. 'No doubt if questioned both of them would claim that the age gap between them isn't important; that they love one another, but somehow such arguments fail to be convincing, and one is always left with the uncomfortable feeling that he has bought her youth to wear on his arm like a trophy and that she has sold herself out to him because it is easier to be the pampered pet of an indulgent older man than to work at a relationship with someone younger and poorer.'

The distaste in his voice echoed his words, causing Hazel to stare at him in surprise.

'You don't agree?' he questioned, watching her.

'Yes . . . yes, as a matter of fact I do,' she told him vehemently when she had got over her surprise. 'It's just that it's so unusual to hear a man voicing such views. A woman, yes, but men seem to have a complete blind spot where their own vanity is concerned. Ask any man of over forty if he genuinely and honestly believes that a girl of eighteen or twenty can really love a man in his fifties for himself and not his assets, and he will immediately say yes, denying every argument you can give him to prove otherwise.'

There was a small pause while they were served with their first course, and when the waiter had gone Silas leaned across the table and said quietly to her, 'You don't have a very high opinion of my sex, do you, Hazel? We aren't all blind to reality, you know. Nor do all of us have such fragile egos that we need to buy ourselves a pretty little plaything to show off to our friends.'

'No, I know,' Hazel agreed. 'That was why I was so upset when I thought that you and Katie——'

She stopped abruptly. Oh, God, what on earth was she saying? But it was too late—after a sharp look at her, Silas was already demanding evenly, 'That Katie and I what, Hazel?'

She cast around desperately in her mind for something innocuous to say, but she could almost feel the seconds ticking by, and with them Silas's patience. She could almost feel the silent pressure of his demand that she answer his question. There was no escape.

Even if she could think of a suitable fib, she knew she just did not have the self-confidence to utter it with any real conviction.

'I assumed . . . that is I thought . . . Well, Katie didn't . . .'

'You thought that Katie and I were lovers,' Silas supplied for her, cutting through her embarrassed attempts to admit how she had misjudged him.

'Well, yes...yes I did, but only because... Well...' She remembered just in time that she was supposed to have extended an invitation to him to stay with her while he was doing his research and realised that she could hardly tell him that when Katie had described him to her in such glowing terms she had quite naturally assumed that Katie was romantically involved with him, not realising that her daughter had simply been trying to prepare the way for her acceptance of him as a potential lodger.

'Because what?' Silas asked her evenly. 'Because I immediately struck you as the type of man who would become involved with a girl as young as Katie? A girl young enough to be my daughter.'

'I... Well...'

He was furious with her and no wonder, she acknowledged wretchedly.

'I can understand why you might think that I might be tempted by a girl of Katie's prettiness and vitality. Just... But what I can't understand is how you could ever have imagined that Katie would be interested in me.'

'Well, I thought... I thought you'd be younger,' she told him defensively.

'Younger.' He was frowning at her. 'I realise the photographs on the back of my dust jackets are somewhat out of date but——'

'And although Katie is very sensible, I thought she might... Well, I worried. Some girls of her age do seem to feel the need for a father figure...'

'Some do,' Silas agreed. 'But not Katie.'

'I'm sorry if I've offended you,' Hazel apologised miserably. Why on earth had she been so stupid? The trouble was that she had been so bemused, so thrown off guard by his contempt for the other couple that she had forgotten to guard her tongue, and had spoken impulsively and from the heart.

'I'm sorry too,' Silas told her, pushing away his food half-eaten.

Hazel discovered that she too had lost her appetite. When the waiter came to remove their plates and serve their main course, he frowned unhappily at their far from empty plates, increasing Hazel's feelings of guilt.

'It never occurred to me that you'd imagine... Katie is a lovely girl, young, pretty, lively and intelligent; the kind of girl it's always a joy to behold from a purely aesthetic point of view, but sexually... She *is* still a girl, but I am not a boy.'

He paused while the waiter served their main course.

Every word he uttered was increasing Hazel's feelings of guilt and shame. If he had lost his temper with her, it would have been easier to bear, but he hadn't done. Instead she could almost feel the distaste and disbelief radiating from him, making her feel guilty of the most gross kind of misjudgement.

Once the waiter had gone, he continued curtly, 'As I was saying, sexually I don't have the remotest interest in Katie... In fact...'

Hazel couldn't look at him. To her horror she could feel tears gathering behind her eyes. Keeping her head lowered towards her plate, she tried frantically to blink them away.

The evening had been disastrous enough as it was, without her adding to its horrors by bursting into tears.

But nothing she could do could stop the tears from welling and rolling slowly down her face. A face which had become so hot from embarrassment and shame that she was only surprised her tears didn't turn into steam from that heat.

She tried to dip her head even lower, but it was too late.

She heard Silas swear under his breath, and then the next thing she knew he was standing up and saying urgently to her, 'Come on, let's get out of here. This is something we need to discuss in private.'

She tried to tell him that there wasn't anything to discuss, but somehow or other she was on her feet, and his arm was round her, guiding her, comforting her almost, certainly shielding her from the potentially curious stares of the other diners.

She heard him saying something to the owner about his wife not feeling well as he paid the bill.

All Hazel wanted was to get out of the restaurant as quickly as she could, and not just out of the restaurant but out of Silas's company as well.

She had embarrassed herself and she had no doubt embarrassed him just as much. What she had said had been bad enough, but to break down in tears like that ...

The cold night air hit her, making her shiver. Immediately Silas put his arm around her, pulling her back into the warmth of his body, his gesture almost an automatic one, as though they were in actual fact a couple and he had held her like this many times before.

'You're cold,' he stated matter of factly. 'Let's get back to the car.'

He had parked a few minutes' walk away, and although Hazel tried discreetly to pull away from him he made no attempt to let her go.

'I'm sorry for behaving like such a fool,' she apologised when they reached the car and Silas opened the passenger door for her.

'Don't apologise,' he told her. 'It was my fault. I upset you.'

'You had every right to be angry with me,' Hazel told him as she closed her door and he got into the car beside her.

'Angry!' He turned to look at her as he fastened his seatbelt, frowning a little. 'I wasn't *angry*. Disappointed, hurt maybe, because I felt you'd misjudged me, but I wasn't angry, Hazel.'

'I shouldn't have said anything. I——'

'I'm glad you did. In fact ...' He paused and looked at her and then asked mildly, 'Does Katie know that you thought she and I were lovers?'

'Yes,' Hazel admitted. 'I couldn't understand why the two of you seemed to want to spend so little time together. She thought it was funny. She wanted to tell you there and then, but...well, I asked her not to.'

She yawned suddenly, overtaken by a wave of emotional and physical exhaustion.

'You're tired,' Silas commented. 'And no wonder, heaving that damned desk around and then getting that bedroom ready for me.'

'I'm thirty-six, not seventy-six,' Hazel retaliated drily.

Silas had been about to start the car's engine, but now he paused and looked at her thoughtfully. 'Do you know, that's the first time I've heard you say something positive about your age? You look younger than many women of thirty, and yet you try desperately hard to give people the impression that you're at least twenty years older than you actually are. All the time in your response to people, you seem to be telling them not that you're a highly desirable woman, but that you're a woman who has put the years of her sexuality behind her. Most women of your age these days would be most affronted if anyone were to suggest that they were sexually past it, so to speak.'

'I'm *not* most women,' Hazel told him stiffly. 'My father——'

'Your father locked you away in an emotional chastity belt, yes, I know,' Silas broke in grittily. 'You were barely sixteen when Katie was conceived. Little more than a baby yourself, and in all the years since her birth I suspect that you've remained as unawakened sexually as you were when she was conceived.'

This wasn't the kind of conversation she ought to be having with him. It was far too dangerous, far too laden with potential hazards.

'If you're going to ask me why I've never made any attempt to experiment sexually, then the answer is that obviously I have a very low, not to say virtually non-existent sex drive,' she told him fiercely, 'and now could we please change the subject? You brought me out to dinner so that we could discuss your book.'

'A very low sex drive,' he repeated musingly, ignoring the latter part of her speech. 'Mm... or perhaps a father who made you feel so guilty and ashamed of your sexuality that you were emotionally coerced into suppressing it.'

'Well it's hardly of world-shattering importance now either way, is it?' Hazel interrupted him. 'After all, at thirty-six I'm hardly likely to——'

'There you go again, Silas told her. 'At thirty-six you're hardly likely to what? Fall in love? Why on earth not? Thousands do... every day.'

'Yes, teenagers. People in their twenties——'

'No,' Silas contradicted her ruthlessly. 'Not just people under thirty. I have an uncle. He never married, never wanted to, and then when he was sixty-five he went on a cruise, met someone, fell in love and married her. They've just celebrated their tenth wedding anniversary and they're as much in love now as they were when they first met, and before you ask, no, she isn't some young girl, in fact Louise is actually three years older than Frank. Before they met she'd had a very hard life, a husband who treated her badly, and then left her with five children to bring up. Those hardships are reflected in her face and it was those, her vulnerabilities as much as her strengths, that drew my uncle to her.

'Love isn't restricted to the very young, Hazel, and why should it be? Isn't it true after all that all too often it's something they take for granted and frequently abuse? Older people can fall in love too, you know.'

'Even those as old as thirty-six,' she said shakily.

'Even those as old as forty-one,' he told her softly, startling her into looking directly into his eyes.

It was a mistake. Her heart missed a beat and then another. She suddenly discovered that it was hard to breathe.

Was Silas going to kiss her, and what if he did? she wondered in panic. Would she be able to stop herself from responding to him? Would she...?

As the frantic thoughts flooded through her head and she tensed her body against them, Silas smiled at her, and then turned the key in the ignition.

He wasn't going to kiss her after all she realised indignantly, trying to tell herself that it wasn't disappointment that she was feeling at all, and that she was glad...yes, glad that he had finally started the engine and put an end to the dangerous conversation they had been having.

As Silas drove out of the town and into the darkness of the surrounding countryside, Hazel yawned again. She felt desperately tired; a legacy from her sleepless nights and emotional turmoil. She leaned her head back against the headrest and closed her eyes. Just for a few minutes. She wasn't going to go to sleep. She was just going to relax, that was all.

Silas glanced at the sleeping figure in the passenger seat, grimacing wryly to himself as he noted the way she had turned her body away from him. Even in her sleep she withdrew from him.

It had stunned him tonight to discover that she had thought he was sexually involved with Katie, but, unflattering though her assumptions had been, they did explain a great deal.

Was he being a complete fool? he wondered musingly, glancing back at her. She certainly wasn't willing to admit him into her life, but she wasn't totally indifferent to him either. Had her father repressed her basic femininity so much that she would never be able to overcome that repression? She had described herself as having a low sex drive. Her body had already given him a very, very different message.

But would she ever be able to accept that . . . that what? That he had virtually fallen in love with her from Katie's description of her, and that his first sight of her had only confirmed what he had already felt? And even if she *accepted* it, would she care?

She had responded to him when he kissed her, but sexual response was not love. He reflected that it was just as well her father *was* dead. They could almost certainly never have been friends. He had damaged her too much, destroyed her self-esteem and hurt her, even if he had not done that damage maliciously or knowingly.

When he stopped the car in the drive, Hazel was still asleep. Getting out of the car, he found the set of keys she had given him and went to open the back door. Then, returning to the car, he opened the passenger door and said her name quietly.

She moved in her sleep, frowning as though she had heard him, but refusing to wake up.

Common sense told him that the sensible thing to do was to give her a little shake and speak more loudly, but when had a man in love ever behaved sensibly, even one of forty-one? Especially one of forty-one, he told himself with a wry smile, as he leaned into the car and released her seatbelt, before gently easing her out of the seat and into his arms.

She weighed less heavily than his teenage god-daughter, but then she was almost half a head shorter as well. His sisters were going to love her. They were always on at him to get married, chivvying him for being too fussy, telling him that he was in danger of turning into a fussy old bachelor.

As he carried her towards the house, she seemed to nestle into his arms, burrowing against his body, making a soft sound of pleasure as she turned her face into his throat.

The sensation of her warm breath against his skin paralysed him where he stood, a wave of intense longing and need sweeping over him, making him wryly aware that falling in love wasn't the only thing that, supposedly reserved for the youthful, could overtake a man of forty-one—but the very worst thing he could do right now would be to sweep her off to bed and make love to her the way his body was so urgently demanding.

Before he even so much as kissed her again, he needed to build up her trust, her self-confidence...he needed to establish a bridge between them, a rapport; he needed to make her respond to him as a fellow human being before he could show her how much he wanted to respond to her as a woman.

Which was why the moment they were inside the kitchen he put her down rather urgently, causing her to wake up abruptly and stare bemusedly into his eyes.

What was happening? Hazel wondered sleepily. What was she doing in the kitchen, standing so close to Silas that she could actually feel his heartbeat, when the last thing she could remember was being in the passenger seat of his car?

She looked away from him to the still open kitchen door. Had she really walked through it without realising what she was doing?

'I carried you in,' Silas told her, answering her unspoken question. 'I tried to wake you, but you were too deeply asleep.'

He had carried her in! She looked up at him, her eyes still dazed with sleep, as her body continued to absorb the warmth of his. She didn't want to move away from him. She wanted to stay right where she was. She wanted...

She looked at his mouth, her own lips parting, unconsciously seeking his kiss. Silas looked back at her, knowing that if he touched her now...

Immediately he stepped back from her and just as immediately Hazel realised what she was doing, what she was inviting. She was practically begging him to kiss her. No wonder he was looking at her so grimly. What on earth must he think of her?

She stepped back from him instinctively, not trusting herself to be able to look at him.

'I'm rather tired,' she told him quickly. 'If you don't mind, I think I'll have an early night.'

It was only later, when she was just on the verge of sleep, that she realised that neither of them had really eaten. For herself the last thing she wanted was food, but Silas...

He was an intelligent adult, she reminded herself. If he wanted something to eat, presumably he would make himself a meal. As she fell asleep, she was smiling a little sadly to herself, remembering her father, who would have been shocked and confused by any suggestion that he might prepare his own meals, but then her father and Silas were two very, very different members of the male sex.

CHAPTER SEVEN

A WEEK passed and then another. Silas was so absorbed in the research on his book that Hazel only saw him in the evening when he joined her for a meal.

She had come to look forward to these shared meals, sometimes prepared by her, sometimes prepared by Silas and sometimes, now that she too was working on a new commission, by them both together. It had amazed her at first that a man could be so masculine and yet at the same time be so at home and at ease domestically. One cold evening when she had made a casserole which was one of Katie's favourites, Silas had enthused over it and asked her for the recipe.

Sometimes he discussed his book with her, outlining to her what he was doing, giving her a fascinating glimpse into the construction based on hard facts that supported the fictional fabric of his work, and then there were other evenings when they barely spoke at all, but when their silences were comfortable and shared.

She had grown too used to having him around in far too short a space of time, she acknowledged one evening when he had telephoned her from Chester to say that he would be staying late at the library, checking up on some reference books he was unable to bring home.

That evening she ate alone and found that she had no appetite for the meal she had prepared; that she was too restless and lonely to settle . . . that the house felt empty without him in it and that she missed him in a way that she had not even missed Katie when she left for university.

He was becoming too important to her, she acknowledged, shivering a little in the chill of that knowledge.

After several days of blustering winds and rain she woke up one morning to discover that the rain had stopped and that the sun was shining, revealing the untidiness of the garden, and pricking her conscience to do something about it.

Silas announced over breakfast that he intended to spend the day visiting several of the area's older houses, in order to do some more research.

'How is your work going?' he asked her, reaching behind him for the coffee jug and filling both their mugs.

'Quite well. I've finished the preliminary sketches. I sent them off yesterday and now I have to wait for the author's reaction.'

'Mm . . . Well, why don't you have a day off and come out with me? I could do with a good navigator.'

She ached to be able to say yes. There was nothing she would enjoy more than spending the day in Silas's company. Unless of course it was spending the night with him . . . She swallowed tensely. She was constantly having to battle against such wayward thoughts, against her growing desire to extend the intimacy of friendship which was growing between them to that of lovers, but since that one time when he had kissed her Silas had been scrupulous about maintaining a physical distance between them. There was nothing now in his manner towards her that suggested he found her remotely desirable as a woman. And that of course was what she wanted... Or at least it was what she had told herself she wanted.

She was not sure she could cope with several hours alone with him in the intimacy of his car. Her sleep last night had been disturbed by a particularly erotic and vivid dream in which he... She swallowed hard.

'I'd love to,' she told him honestly. 'But I've promised myself that I'll do some work in the garden while it's dry.'

Silas looked towards the window.

'The forecast is quite good for the next few days. Why not put it off until the weekend? I should be able to take a break then and we can do the gardening together.'

Together... What a wonderful word that was. She was desperately tempted to give in, to say yes, to ignore all those small warning voices clamouring so urgently inside her. What, after all, did it matter if Silas realised she wanted him?

It mattered a great deal, she told herself severely. He would find her desire for him embarrassing; it would spoil the friendship which was growing between them.

Regretfully she shook her head. 'No. I really ought to make a start today.'

She waited, telling herself that if he pressed her... already half regretting having refused him, but he simply drank his coffee and said easily, 'Well, if I can't persuade you to join me I suppose. I'd still better make a move.'

Half an hour later, as he left, he gave her another cheerful smile, leaving her with no idea that his whole purpose in asking her to join him had not been because of any research he wanted to do, but because he had hoped that the intimacy of being completely alone with her might allow him to take their relationship a step further.

Outside, away from the domestic setting of the house, there would have been far more opportunities to begin a subtle physical bonding with her. After all he could hardly put his arm around her to help her walk across the kitchen... at least not at this stage of their relationship.

And now he had condemned himself to spending a whole day away from her, supposedly doing some quite unnecessary research. So much for the table he had surreptitiously booked for lunch. So much for all the plans he had so carefully been laying. Wouldn't it, he wondered wryly, be far easier and more adult to simply tell her how he felt and to invite her to either accept or reject him?

Easier perhaps, but he was not sure that she would take him seriously. It was true that she had ceased mentioning her age, as though it were some kind of barrier to her either feeling or engendering in someone else sexual desire, but he was still not sure if she would want to accept that he found her physically desirable to such an extent that there were times when it took every ounce of will-power he possessed to stop himself from reaching out and taking hold of her.

Unenthusiastically, Hazel went upstairs and changed into an old pair of jeans and a thick sweater.

In the kitchen she pulled on her wellingtons and a sleeveless jacket and, picking up her gardening gloves, opened the back door. The sun might be shining but the wind was cold, though digging over the vegetable patch ought to warm her up a bit.

Three hours later, her back aching and her energy flagging, she acknowledged that she had had enough. But it was still only lunchtime and Silas would be gone all day. She felt reluctant to go back into the empty house, but she was certainly not in the mood for any more gardening. Her muscles ached for the comfort of a hot bath, and then perhaps afterwards she could light the sitting-room fire and curl up in a chair there with a book.

Telling herself that what she was contemplating was the grossest self-indulgence, she cleared the clogging mud off her tools and returned them to the shed before walking tiredly towards the house.

Outside she removed her wellingtons and padded across the kitchen floor, stripping off her jeans and top where she stood, to stuff them into the washing machine with a grimace of distaste.

Upstairs in the bathroom, she ran a deep, hot bath, and added a liberal amount of the bath oil Katie had given her for her birthday, breathing in its heady fragrance with enjoyment.

Securing her curls on top of her head with an elasticated silky band which had originally belonged to Katie, she sank blissfully into the water.

Less than five miles away, Silas stared moodily into his driving mirror. What the hell was he doing driving around aimlessly like this when the only place he really wanted to be was at home with Hazel?

Stopping abruptly, and checking the empty road, he swung the car round. Hazel might not want to be with him, but he certainly wanted to be with her... needed to be with her.

Downstairs the phone rang. Hazel heard it but ignored it, but when it continued to ring all her maternal instincts were activated and she clambered out of the bath, telling herself that it probably wasn't Katie telephoning her at all, and that even if she was it didn't necessarily mean that there was something wrong.

Nevertheless she reached for a towel, and then cursed mildly under her breath, remembering that she had left the clean towels neatly folded in the kitchen.

In her father's day the very last thing she would have been able to do was what she was doing now, which was hurrying downstairs, naked and damp, grateful for the warmth of the house's central heating and reflecting that there were after all some advantages to living on one's own.

As she picked up the receiver in the hallway, she told herself that one day soon she really must buy herself a modern remote control phone which she could take into the bathroom with her.

'Ma.'

'Katie, it *is* you. What's wrong? Is——?'

'Nothing's wrong. Heavens, you do panic. I've got a free period and I thought I'd give you a ring. I haven't disturbed anything important, have I?'

'I was in the bath,' Hazel told her, 'and right now I'm standing in the hall, dripping water all over the place.'

'Mm...I take it that you're all alone then, and that there's no Silas there to appreciate the view,' Katie teased her.

'Silas has gone out for the day,' Hazel told her repressively. 'Is everything all right, Katie?'

'Everything's fine. As a matter of fact, I rang because *I* was worried about *you*. Is everything OK with you and Silas? I mean, are the two of you getting on all right?'

'Yes, yes we're getting on fine,' Hazel told her, frowning as she thought she heard the sound of a car drawing up outside.

'Katie, I'm going to have to go. I think some-one's outside——' she began. Before she could re-place the receiver, Katie called out urgently, 'Hang on a sec, Ma. I think I'll be coming home for Christmas on about the twentieth.'

Hazel froze as she heard the kitchen door open. She had locked it when she came in, she knew she had, and besides she didn't know anyone who would just walk in without knocking, apart from Silas, and he...and he...

Her jaw dropped as the hall door opened and Silas walked through it.

For the space of a heartbeat, they both stood looking at one another, and Hazel had never felt more vulnerable, nor more of a fool in her entire life. Humiliatingly, Silas seemed to be deliberately avoiding looking directly at her, and no wonder, she thought wretchedly, as she said jerkily to Katie, 'Yes, yes, that's fine, Katie. I must go. I . . .'

Silas mercifully had gone back into the kitchen. Why on earth hadn't she gone and got a towel instead of coming downstairs like that? Why hadn't she . . . what? Guessed that he would come back?

She had just replaced the receiver and was about to go upstairs when the kitchen door opened again. She froze where she stood.

'Here, I've brought you this,' Silas told her quietly.

He was holding out a clean towel to her, one of the ones she had earlier removed from the dryer and folded prior to taking them upstairs.

'Thanks,' she responded tightly, reaching for it, without daring to look at him, but somehow it slipped from her fingers and as both of them moved forward together to pick it up, Hazel felt herself start to tremble when Silas's fingers brushed against hers. She straightened up abruptly, and then winced as something tugged sharply at her hair.

'Hang on,' she heard Silas saying above her in a muffled voice. 'You seem to have got caught. You'll have to move a little closer to me,' he told her as she tried to move and realised that her hair had managed to entwine itself around one of his shirt buttons as they had both reached down for the towel.

There was nothing she could do other than stand there, every inch of her bare skin burning with mortification and embarrassment, as Silas painstakingly unravelled the snarled-up curl from around his button.

It seemed to take forever, and, even though she knew that his gaze was fixed on his task, Hazel was agonisingly conscious of her nudity.

What on earth had made her come downstairs like that in the first place? It wasn't something she would normally have done. In fact there were often occasions when Katie had teased her about being over modest, informing her vehemently, 'Honestly, Ma, you ought to be proud of your body, not always trying to hide it away. You've got a terrific figure. And you know what they say, don't you? If you've got it, flaunt it.'

Well, she had certainly taken her daughter's advice to heart today, she reflected shakily. What on earth must Silas think of her? Did he imagine that she was trying to be deliberately provocative, that she was...?

She gave a tiny shiver of distress, and immediately Silas said huskily, 'I'm sorry. You're cold. You're nearly free.'

He was sorry! It was her fault she was in this situation, not his. She wondered what he would say if she told him that she hadn't been shivering because she was cold, but because she was realising that no matter how much she might protest it with her conscious mind, subconsciously it had been that wanton, dangerous streak within her which was responsible for her present plight.

She shivered again, her embarrassment giving way to the beginnings of a definite erotic tension; an awareness that, despite the fact that he was fully clothed, Silas's body was the male counterpart to her own femininity. She could feel the heat his flesh was generating and trembled violently in response to it. She heard Silas curse, and then suddenly she was free and able to step back from him.

As he bent to retrieve her towel, she saw that his hand was trembling slightly.

'I'm sorry,' she apologised huskily.

He paused in the act of handing her the towel, his gaze locking with hers. His eyes burned with an unfamiliar heat that made her own pulses race.

'What for?' he demanded rawly. 'For letting me see you like this?'

The way he looked at her then made her feel more conscious of herself as a woman than she had ever felt in her whole life; not self-conscious and uncomfortable with her sexuality, not ashamed and guilty about her body, but somehow proud of her femininity, aware of its power and strength, aware of herself as the focus of male desire.

In that second an avalanche of sensations and emotions came crashing down over her, the burden of years of self-repression falling away from her so that she was conscious of herself and her needs so sharply that that awareness was almost a physical pain.

She took a step towards him, ignoring the towel, impulsively wanting to share with him the wonder of what she was feeling, and then abruptly he killed that impulse by adding violently, 'Yes, Hazel, so am I.'

She froze where she stood, all her self-doubts and fears coming crowding back, and added to them was an extra burden of humiliation and shame. Of course he didn't want her. Of course he hadn't been implying...

She started to shake violently, tears burning the back of her throat.

'Hazel, what is it? What's wrong?'

Her emotions were too strong to allow her to speak. He was still holding the towel and suddenly to her surprise he held it open and said softly, 'Come here—let's get you wrapped up in this before my self-control deserts me completely. Have you any idea what you're doing to me?' he demanded huskily, as he enveloped her in the towel, somehow or other drawing her closer to him as he did so, so that when he picked her up, lifting her completely off her feet and cradling her in his arms, she had no option but to let him do so, wrapping her arms instinctively around his neck for additional security as he headed for the stairs.

'You and I need to talk,' he told her quietly as he climbed the stairs.

'I'm sorry if I gave you a shock coming back so unexpectedly like that, but I didn't...'

Hazel wriggled uncomfortably in his arms, guessing what he had been about to say, but unable to put it into words. Of course he hadn't expected to walk in and find her standing in the hall without a stitch on.

They were at the top of the stairs now and he was heading in the direction of her bedroom.

'I want to talk to you, but not while you're like this.'

Of course not. Her face burned. Did he suspect that she had done it deliberately? But how could he? *She* hadn't known he would come back.

He was just about to put her down on the bed when she felt the tension in his arms. Her own muscles locked in mute response as she looked towards his downbent head.

'Hazel.'

He said her name on a rough, long drawn out breath that brushed her skin with warmth and turned her body liquid.

As he gently unfastened the towel and kissed the hollow between her breasts, she shivered with shocked delight, the hands which she had locked behind his neck for support developing a will and an instinct of their own so that they spread across his shoulders, stroking the hard muscles, her soft murmur of pleasure breaking the thick silence of the room.

As though that sound held some special plea, some secret message, Silas sat down on the bed, still cradling her to him, his lips exploring the soft swell of one breast, while his hands gently cupped and held their roundness.

Now the silence of the room was splintered not just by the accelerated sound of her own breathing but by Silas's as well. With hearing that was suddenly preternaturally sharp she could hear the soft sound of his mouth moving against her skin, could feel its sensual vibration deep within her body, could feel a growing urgent desire to hold him close to her, to arch her back, and wantonly invite him to stroke every inch of her exposed skin with the same wonderful sensuality with which he was caressing her breasts.

It was the most erotic sensation she had experienced in her life, and the most dangerous, but she ignored the danger, letting herself be swept away on the turbulent mill-race of sensations flooding through her.

And when Silas did slide the towel from her body, lingering, caressing her skin with the silken warmth of his mouth, it was like a dream come true, like a private secret fantasy, too magical surely to be actually happening.

The soft sounds of her wonderment and pleasure seemed to be all the encouragement he needed, and when his lips finally, tenderly possessed the eager excitement of her tautly erect nipple, the little whimpers of shocked delight she tried to strangle in her throat caused him to draw the hot, aching nub of flesh fully into his mouth and to draw on it so erotically that the sensation made her cry out loud in shocked recognition of her own need.

Immediately she made that high keening sound, Silas's hands—which had been caressing the slender roundness of her hips, stimulating her sensitive flesh so that her whole body quivered with responsiveness to him—stilled, just as his mouth ceased caressing her breast.

Bewilderment, anger, disbelief, but most of all anguished humiliation swept through her as he slowly withdrew from her, silently re-covering her with her towel, his glance fixed on a point somewhere beyond her shoulder as he said roughly, 'I'm sorry. I should never...' He got up, moving away from her, while she lay on her bed, frozen with misery and rejection, not knowing what she had said or done to provoke his withdrawal from her.

'I...I have to go out,' he told her quietly. 'I'm not sure when I'll be back.'

Unable to move, to speak, to do anything other than simply close her eyes on the anguish she was feeling, Hazel heard him go.

Even when she had heard the sound of his car engine fading away, she still dared not allow herself to breathe properly, still dared not allow herself to move.

Inside her body ached tormentingly, adding to the burdens of self-contempt and shock she was already carrying.

Dear God, how could she have behaved like that? How could she have been so...so wanton? And when she had already told him that she didn't want him.

Well, he knew the truth now. Knew that she had lied. No wonder he had withdrawn from her in such disgust.

Shakily she got off the bed, her body weak and drained, her hands trembling as she dressed herself.

What would have happened if he hadn't stopped when he had? If he, like her, had been so overwhelmed by need, by desire. By love!

She sat down on her bed, covering her face with her hands, her body shaking with silent sobs of despair as she acknowledged the truth.

She had fallen in love with Silas. It wasn't simply desire that motivated her. It wasn't simply some belated awakening of her senses, of her desires, responding to the proximity of a very attractive male.

She had fallen in love. Vividly she recalled the first moment she had seen him, the emotions she had felt then—had felt and had tried to suppress, believing that he and Katie were lovers. It was too late now to wish she had never met him; to wish that what she was feeling now had remained something she had never experienced.

Her burgeoning emotions were a thousand times more painful than the most acute attack of pins and needles, tormenting her into an agony of misery and depression.

It was a long time before she felt able to go downstairs. Her body felt oddly weak, and yet at the same time she was acutely conscious of how it still ached, still yearned.

When Silas did not return for supper, she realised that he was trying to keep as much distance between them as he could. She went to bed early, determined to do the same, but she couldn't sleep. She heard him come in when the hands of her alarm clock showed the time at just gone midnight. Where had he been? Had he been alone?

Jealousy ate into her like acid fire, showing her yet another hitherto unknown side of her nature. It was a long, long time before she managed to get to sleep.

For three days they continued to avoid one another, meeting briefly in the kitchen in the morning over breakfast, when she was meticulous about responding to whatever conversational comments Silas made to her with monosyllabic answers and an averted profile. It was far too late for her to do anything about the fact that he must be aware of her desire for him, but at least she could salvage something of her pride by ensuring that that was all he knew... by keeping herself aloof, and showing him that no matter what her weaknesses might be she was adult enough to control and withstand them. And yet just to see him, just to hear his voice, just to know he was in the house with her, caused the most idiotic and useless weakening within her, the most appalling, yearning desire.

If this was love, she had been better off when she had had no knowledge of it, she decided bitterly one morning as she parked her car and headed for the supermarket entrance, her heart sinking as she was immediately hailed by Sheila Simpson.

Sheila Simpson was the very last person she felt like speaking to today. All she really wanted was to be left alone. To wallow in her misery and self-pity? She smiled bitterly to herself.

'My goodness, you are a dark horse, aren't you?' Sheila exclaimed archly as she caught up with her. 'When I asked if you were expecting guests, I had no idea ... I mean I assumed ...'

Hazel focused on her, her eyes blank with dismissal.

'What exactly is it you're trying to imply, Sheila?' she asked almost sharply. Where once she would have been upset and embarrassed to confront Sheila and demand an explanation of what she was attempting to say, suddenly she felt no such restrictions. She was, after all, an adult woman, not a child. She was responsible to no one other than herself. Her father was no longer alive to be upset by any kind of reference to her sexuality.

'Well, nothing,' Sheila backtracked, looking slightly ruffled. 'But if you *will* have a man living with you, you have to expect that people will assume——'

'Will assume what?' she demanded coolly. 'That we're lovers?'

Sheila flushed unflatteringly. 'Well, yes,' she agreed, looking uncomfortable. 'Of course I've said that there's no truth in that kind of gossip. But you know what people are...'

'I know what *some* people are,' Hazel agreed pointedly, sweeping past her, as she added acidly, 'And now, if you'll excuse me, Sheila, I really must get on with my shopping.'

It was only when she was halfway down the aisle with her shopping trolley that she realised that she was still trembling. You're over-reacting, she warned herself, but that warning did no good. She wasn't used to being the object of people's prurient speculation and curiosity and she discovered that she did not care for the idea that she might be.

She loathed the thought of people talking about her and Silas—discussing them with the same kind of cynical destructive cruelty with which she had heard them discussing others. It made her feel besmirched, dirty—it made her feel... She shook her head, telling herself she was behaving like a fool, but the feelings of anger and misery Sheila's comments had caused refused to go away. They were still with her several hours later, when Silas walked into the kitchen just when she was in the middle of preparing supper.

The unexpectedness of seeing him, when she had grown accustomed to his spending most of the day away from the house, made her freeze.

'Is something wrong?' he queried frowningly, looking at her.

'I just wasn't expecting to see you.'

'No, I can see that,' he agreed, and there was a note in his voice that made her tense even more, a bitter, almost derisory note that was so unlike his normal manner that it was as abrasive, as harsh as sandpaper against her sensitive nerves.

'I came back because there's something I want to tell you.'

She stopped what she was doing and watched him. Her heart was already beating far too fast. She was aware of a sensation of doom, of misery hanging over her. She wanted to stop him from speaking, from telling her whatever it was he wanted to say, because she knew already that it was something she did not want to hear.

'I've found somewhere else to stay.'

He said it abruptly, challengingly almost, so that the shock of it was increased.

She couldn't speak, couldn't react at all, other than to stare at him in stunned silence.

'It seemed to be the best thing to do in the circumstances,' he added roughly when she didn't respond. 'I'll move my stuff out this evening.'

Hazel knew she ought to say something, make some response, but she simply could not trust herself to speak. If she did she was terrified that she would simply go to pieces and break down completely, but she had to say something, had to pretend that she didn't care, that she didn't mind—that he wasn't tearing her heart apart. The habits of a lifetime, ingrained so deeply by her father, flooded through her now, and she heard herself saying in an unfamiliar, metallic-clad voice, 'I won't make you any supper, then.'

The banality of what she was saying made her want to scream out loud with hysteria, but somehow she just managed to restrain herself, to stop herself from doing so.

Silas was going, leaving. And it was all her fault. All her fault. If she hadn't reacted like a fool—if she hadn't shown him so plainly how totally besotted she was with him... But what was the point of berating herself now? What was the point of trying to cling on? Where was her pride, her self-sufficiency? Where was her backbone?

CHAPTER EIGHT

IT WAS a question she was forced to ask herself over and over again in the twenty-four hours that followed, and she was forced to watch in silence while Silas loaded his things into his car, and then gravely sought her out to thank her for everything she had done for him.

Just before he left, he moved towards her, almost as though he was going to take her in his arms, but immediately he checked the gesture, turning on his heel and leaving without even saying a formal goodbye.

She waited until she was sure he had gone before giving way to her grief. Not in floods of tears, but in a silent anguished agony, which had her curling her body into a tightly withdrawn ball and rocking it silently back and forth as she tried to find some means of easing the agony she was suffering.

Just before he had left, Silas had given her his address, just in case, he had told her, she needed to get in touch with him for anything.

He was apparently renting an empty cottage several miles away in a small village.

He had paused just before he left, as though there was something he wanted to say to her, but she had turned her back on him, and so he had gone.

What after all could he have to offer her apart from his pity, which was the last thing she wanted?

It took her three days to pull herself together sufficiently to return to her work, albeit in a lacklustre, unenthusiastic manner, but it was marginally better than lying in bed for half the day, unwilling to open her eyes and face up to life, and then staying up until well into the early hours because she was too emotionally wrought up to sleep.

What she needed, she told herself, was a simple but strict routine, rather like someone recovering from an extremely debilitating illness, which was after all what she was doing, wasn't it? Only as far as she could see recovery was still merely an impossible chimera—the best she could hope for was simply to exist.

She was glad that Katie hadn't telephoned. She didn't think she would be able to conceal her emotional condition from her daughter, and the last thing she wanted was to upset or worry her, and then, three days after Silas had left, and just as she was promising herself that this evening she would have her supper, do some work on her latest commission and then go to bed at a reasonable time, she heard a car pulling up outside.

Her senses were so acutely attuned that they recognised the sound of Silas's car engine immediately.

Telling herself that it was impossible, that he couldn't have come back, she tensed, staring avidly at the back door.

When she saw his familiar shape passing the kitchen window, she panicked and would have turned and fled if he hadn't already seen her.

When he knocked on the door she went slowly to open it, and then stood there speechless with anguish, with the pain of loving him, with all the things she was experiencing at far too late a stage in her life for her ever to be able to recover from the anguish of the experience.

Her first thought that he must have forgotten something made her stand to one side to let him in.

It must be the quality of the late autumn dusk that made his skin look so pale and his face so drawn, she told herself as he came into the kitchen.

'I was hoping I'd catch you in,' was his initial comment. He wasn't looking directly at her, and in another man she would have put his hesitation, his tension down to nervousness, but Silas had never betrayed such an emotion to her before, and she could only think that this visit was a reluctant one, paid out of necessity; a chore he wished to get over as quickly as possible. What did he fear—that she would lose control completely and fling herself at him, begging him to want her, to love her?

Her self-disgust, never far from the surface these days, welled up sickeningly inside her.

How well now she understood the description 'lovesick'.

She had thought it was an affliction reserved for teenagers, but she was discovering just how wrong she had been.

'Are you doing anything this evening?'

Silas's question, raw, jerky, and delivered in a manner so abruptly different from his normal easy, pleasant style, made her raise surprised eyes to his face, and reply without thinking.

'No, not really. I had intended to do some work but——'

'Good, then you'll be free to have dinner with me.'

Again the way he cut through her hesitant sentence was out of character, just like the tension she could almost feel emanating from him.

'There's something I need to discuss with you,' he added curtly.

Her heart pounded frantically. What did he need to discuss with her? Did he feel that it wasn't enough to have moved out of her house; that he had to explain verbally as well that he didn't want her? Did he think she was a complete fool?

'I don't think——'

I don't think that's necessary, she had been about to say, but once again he didn't let her finish, saying almost pleadingly, 'Hazel, please...I wouldn't normally pressure you like this, but it *is* important.'

What could she say?

'Well...well, if you insist,' she responded doubtfully.

'Good. I'll wait here, shall I, while you get ready?'

He'd *wait*? She stared at him. It was barely six o'clock. It wouldn't take her much more than half an hour to get washed and changed. She had no idea where he intended to take her, but surely it was still a little early to be thinking of going out for dinner? Unless of course it was more that he wished to get the whole thing over and done with as quickly as possible.

'Well, if that's what you want.'

She gave him a questioning, uncertain look to which he responded with a smile so warm, so tender almost, that it rocked her whole nervous system.

Like someone under a powerful spell, she walked blindly towards the door and had opened it and was halfway up the stairs before she realised that she hadn't even asked him where he was taking her.

She told herself recklessly that if she was going to have to sit opposite him and listen to him while he told her that he had guessed her secret and that for both their sakes he felt he must tell her that there was no possibility of his ever returning her love, she might as well do so looking her best, looking like a woman who might potentially excite a man's desire rather that one who already knew deep within herself that she had been rejected, emotionally, sexually, every way by the only man she had ever loved.

To this end, she showered quickly and then dressed determinedly in the satin teddy which Katie had bought her the previous Christmas, claiming that it was the sort of thing that every woman ought to have in her wardrobe.

'But it's wasted on me,' Hazel had protested, and as she had said the words an expression of such anger and compassion had crossed her daughter's face that she had immediately felt seared by the pain of her own lack of sexuality.

'When you do wear it—and you will,' Katie had threatened her, 'make sure you wear it next to your skin with nothing on underneath it.'

Then she had been shocked, repudiating such a suggestion with all the prissiness her father would have approved, but now recklessly she rejected the idea of redonning her bra, and instead slid the cool, silky fabric on to her body, shivering a little as its sensual glide reminded her of Silas's touch.

Stop that, she warned herself, pulling on the silk stockings that went with it, and then wondering with wry self-mockery why she was going to so much trouble for a man who was going to tell her that he was rejecting the sexuality she was finding within herself so late in her life that it was almost as though its discovery was fate's cruel way of deliberately mocking her.

Unsure of exactly where it was Silas intended to take her, and aware that he was downstairs waiting for her, she couldn't dawdle over what to wear, and selected a bright red sweater dress that she had bought several winters previously and then discarded as being too eye-catching for her to wear successfully.

It had a neat round neckline, long sleeves, and a hemline which came sensibly down to mid-knee, and yet despite all these features it still somehow or other contrived to have what Katie referred to as 'oomph'.

The oomph in this case was probably supplied by the row of tiny buttons that went from the throat all the way down past her waist and which were secured with small scarlet loops.

When she had complained, honestly bewildered by her daughter's comment, to Katie that she could not see why her daughter considered the dress so sexy, all Katie had been able to say was 'It's the buttons—there's something about them that no red-blooded male will be able to resist.'

As she remembered this comment, when she was halfway through fastening them, she hesitated, her skin flushing uncomfortably. Was she being totally honest with herself? *Had* she really accepted that Silas didn't want her?

This dress, her underwear, wasn't some kind of foolish last-ditch attempt to make him aware of her, to make him want her... was it?

As she hesitated, torn between tearing off what she was wearing and reverting to her normal far more sensible attire, she heard Silas moving about downstairs, and the decision was made for her. She didn't have time to undress, find fresh clothes and redress. Silas was obviously impatient to get the whole thing over and done with, and who could blame him?

Before going downstairs, she reached into her wardrobe and withdrew a long black woollen jacket, which she pulled on over the dress, taking refuge in its anonymity and dullness.

Silas glanced up at her when she walked into the kitchen, but there was nothing in his expression to suggest that he was the slightest bit interested in whatever she chose to wear. He looked more like a man carrying a very, very heavy burden, a burden which was occupying his thoughts and emotions to the exclusion of everything else.

When they left the house, he was as meticulously polite as always, opening the car door for her, and settling her inside, but sensitively Hazel noticed that it was as though he could barely bring himself to touch her—as though almost he was actually frightened of doing so.

And no wonder, she derided herself bitterly, her face growing hot with embarrassment and guilt when she remembered the abandoned way she had responded to him, the wanton way she had actually not just encouraged but mutely pleaded with him for him to continue caressing her, to touch her more and more intimately.

Lost in these uncomfortable reminiscences, she wriggled self-consciously in her seat, keeping her gaze fixed firmly on the darkness outside the passenger window.

She felt Silas getting into the car beside her. The door slammed and he started the engine, but resolutely she refused to give in to the temptation to turn her head and avidly study him, storing up additional memories of him to savour and cherish for the times when she would be alone. What was the point anyway in such reckless self-punishment?

As she sat motionless in the car beside him, staring out into the darkness, she had no awareness of where they were going, only of the miles slipping past, so that it came as a shock when he drove into a small village and started to slow down, stopping the car outside one of a small row of cottages.

When she turned her head to look at him, he read the question in her eyes and said simply, 'What I want to say to you isn't going to be easy. Selfishly I felt it might be best said in privacy.'

Her stomach muscles clenched, her emotions plummeting downwards in chagrin and misery.

What did he think she was likely to do? Create a scene, demand that he return her love? She suppressed a desire to burst into anguished laughter, to tell him that there was no need to prolong their mutual discomfort; that she already knew exactly what it was he wanted to say and that he need have no fears. She might not be able to control what she felt; she might not be able to root out and destroy the unwanted and stubbornly resistant love for him growing inside her, but she could and would ensure that he wasn't embarrassed by it. But Silas was already climbing out of the car and coming round to open the door for her and she had no option but to walk in silence through the small gate and down the narrow path that led to the cottage's front door.

Inside, Silas had to duck his head to avoid colliding with the low threshold to the sitting-room.

The room was shabbily and anonymously furnished, but at least there was a warm fire burning in the grate, softening the austerity of its unadorned walls.

'I haven't had much time to do anything with it as yet,' Silas was telling her, as though sensing her unspoken criticisms. 'As it was I was lucky to be able to find somewhere like this to rent. Apparently its owner died last year and the son who inherited it hasn't been able to decide whether to sell or to keep it, and let it out to provide income.

'We'll have to eat in the kitchen, and I'm afraid it in no way compares with your kitchen. It's very basic and bare. I miss coming downstairs to the warmth of your Aga in the morning and I suspect I'm going to miss it even more as winter rolls on.'

It was on the tip of her tongue to say that if he missed the Aga that much he could always come back, but her pride stopped her. It would be a stupid thing to say, and pointless as well.

Instead, she told him abruptly and honestly, 'I'm sorry, but I don't think I want anything to eat. You said you needed to talk to me. Couldn't we just...?'

She stopped, and looked away from him, unable to continue.

'If that's what you'd prefer,' he agreed gravely. 'Come and sit down.'

Assuming that he would opt to sit in the larger of the two fireside chairs, she headed for the other, and promptly walked full tilt into him, so that of course his arms came out automatically, to fend her off, or so she thought, until they suddenly closed around her with such force, such violence almost that she breathed out far more sharply than normal and looked up at him.

'I'm sorry. I'm sorry,' he told her rawly, 'but this is killing me, Hazel. Wanting you, needing you, aching for you so much that I'm damn nearly going out of my mind with thinking about you, and all the time tied by that damned promise I gave you that I wouldn't touch you while I was living under your roof—but I'm not living there any longer, and you can tell me to stop if you want to. You can tell me that you don't want this, that you don't want me...'

His body was shaking with emotion and intensity, sending violent answering tremors zigzagging through her own. She was, she discovered, holding on to him as tightly as he was holding her, raising her mouth for the kiss she knew he was going to give her, and, when it came, opening herself to its passion, its need so completely that she felt Silas groaning his pleasure into her mouth as he kissed her and kissed her over and over again as though he simply could not get enough of her.

Dimly she was conscious of him sliding her jacket off her shoulders, and then moulding her against his body, a body which she could tell now was openly aroused, pulsing hard and male, when he slid impatient hands down over her back until he was cupping her bottom and urging her so intimately against him, moving so erotically against her, that it was her turn to gasp and shudder, to cling helplessly to him, letting him mould her to him as though she was as pliant as silk.

'I love you, you know that, don't you?' he was muttering against her throat. 'I think I fell in love with you the very first time Katie started telling me about you. "Come home with me and meet her in person, if you're so fascinated by my mother," she teased me. "She's one of your greatest fans and I know she'd love to meet you." I persuaded myself that it was just because I needed somewhere to stay while I did my research. I told myself that the woman who sounded so entrancing, so...so different when described by her daughter, could hardly turn out to be the same in the flesh, and then I saw you and I realised that nothing Katie had said about you had been an exaggeration. You were...you are perfection.'

He felt her shake, and cupped her face, so that he could look into her eyes.

'Don't you dare laugh at me,' he told her fiercely. 'All right, so I know I'm making a fool of myself; that men of my age simply do not fall so deeply in love that they're incapable of doing anything other than fulfilling that love, but that *doesn't* mean that what I'm feeling is any the less painful. Just because it's ridiculous...'

Hazel stopped him, putting her fingers against his lips. 'I wasn't laughing,' she told him huskily. 'Silas, you don't understand...'

She stopped, still too shy, too insecure, too uncertain to go on, looking at him instead with all that she was feeling revealed in her eyes.

He looked back at her. She heard him catch his breath and then suddenly he was kissing her again. Not this time with intensity, with ferocity, but with slow, gentle tenderness, with adoration as well as need, with... with love, she recognised dreamily as she responded to what he was showing her, letting him see in turn how much he meant to her.

'Is this real?' he demanded huskily, reluctantly releasing her mouth and cradling her against him. 'I feel as if I've stepped into an impossible dream. I brought you here tonight to try to talk to you, to begin to woo you, if you like. To show you that there *could* be something between us, that I *was* capable of behaving with restraint, of curbing my passion, my need, my love, to allow you time to get to know me, and hopefully to come to love me. I thought I'd ruined my chances for ever the other day, but the sight of your naked body, the feel of you in my arms, the sound of your response to me...'

He gave a violent shudder, his eyes suddenly turning dark.

'Have you any idea what you do to me?' he whispered against her ear.

'I think so,' Hazel told him shyly, 'and if it's anything like what you do to me——'

He let her go so abruptly that she almost fell.

'You want me?' he demanded roughly.

'Isn't it obvious that I do?' Hazel retorted.

The smile he gave her made her flush a little. It was full of tenderness and love.

'No,' he told her wryly. 'Oh, yes, I knew that you were responding to me, but I also knew that you were a woman who had never been allowed to develop her sexuality, to appreciate her sensuality...'

'You mean you thought I'd probably have reacted like that to any man who happened to touch me?' Hazel responded, aggrieved.

He laughed a little.

'Not exactly. But you'd already made it obvious that you didn't welcome any physical intimacy between us, and then I'd gone and given you that idiotic promise that I wouldn't touch you while I was living with you...

'Getting this place became essential after the other day. I knew then there was no way I could stay with you and keep that promise, and I was terrified that if I broke it it would mean the end of whatever slender chance I might have of getting you to see me as a human being who had fallen desperately in love with you, rather than simply some man who wanted sex from you.'

'I'm sorry,' Hazel apologised, sensing the pain in his voice. 'But you see I just don't have the experience to tell the difference.'

'I know that, my love.'

He drew her to him again, holding her tenderly. She was so bemused that she could hardly think. Silas loved her. Silas loved her... It seemed impossible but it wasn't.

She was still unsure of herself, though, still painfully aware of her shortcomings.

'You don't mind, then? That I'm not...that I haven't...that I don't have the kind of sexual skill and knowledge that a woman of my age should have?' she managed to finish jerkily.

There was a long silence and then Silas cupped her face, turning her to look directly at him.

'I love *you*,' he told her firmly. 'And that means I love each and every single minute component that goes up to making you the person you are. While I might and do deplore the way your father prevented you from exploring your own sexuality, and the burden of guilt he made you carry, it's you, the person you are, whom I love, and that has nothing to do with any spurious sexual skill, or lack of it. You can turn me on more intensely, simply by being in the same room with me, than could the skills of the world's most experienced courtesan. Come here and let me show you what I mean.'

She was trembling as he drew her even closer to his body, but not with fear...not even with apprehension.

While he kissed her, and she clung eagerly to the sweet magic of his kisses woven on her senses, she could feel his hands trembling over the tiny buttons that closed her dress. When he had opened them as far as her breasts, he groaned and buried his mouth in the soft warm hollow between them, telling her hoarsely, 'You can't know how much I wanted to do this again.'

She was trembling uncontrollably now, hardly able to speak as she told him, 'I know how much *I've* wanted you to do it, though.'

It was as though she had turned a key in a secret lock, as though her words had unleashed a powerful magical force within both of them, so that her inexperience, the long years of celibacy, might never have been, and immediately her body, her senses, her emotions were so responsive to his that each touch, each kiss, each murmured word of praise and longing increased her awareness of her own sensuality, of her body's female strength, of her age-old ability to please this man whom she loved so deeply, to pleasure him, just as he was pleasuring her, with her hands, with her mouth, with her voice as she whispered to him her delight, her need, her love, her pleasure in his body and her own, and finally with the whole of her body, as he drew her down on the floor beside the fire, studying her in silence, before his hands drifted over her naked fire-gilded body, stroking it into liquid silken eager responsiveness so that when he finally entered her her response to him was so immediate, so powerful that, even as she wrapped her legs around him, even as she arched and told him beseechingly how much she wanted him, how much she loved him, how much she needed the sensation of his flesh moving so powerfully, so deeply within her own, pleasure coalesced and built up into such a fiery core that its implosion within her made her tense and cry out in shocked awe, her senses totally unprepared for the awesomeness of so much pleasure.

While her body shook with the shock of so intense an emotional and physical completion, Silas held her tenderly, whispering reassuringly to her that there would be time enough later for him to achieve the same ecstatic state, that there would be all the time in the world for them to share and explore their physical desire for one another, just as they would share and explore their love.

He wanted her for ever, he told her, not just for today, for tonight, but for ever, and he hoped that she wanted him in the same way.

She did, Hazel assured him shakily.

'Enough to marry me?' he asked her gravely.

And it was only then, when she looked at him and saw the uncertainty, the need in his eyes, that she actually did realise that in his love for her he was just as vulnerable as she was herself.

'Yes,' she told him equally gravely. 'Enough for that, and to spare.'

They were married just before Christmas, the quiet church ceremony they had planned somehow becoming a large joint family celebration.

All Silas's family were there, and on an impulse she couldn't really name Hazel had invited Jimmy's mother, all his brothers and sisters, and their children as well.

As Katie happily told anyone who would listen to her, *she* was the one who was responsible for this marriage. She had known from the moment she set eyes on Silas that he was exactly right for her mother, and as she had already fondly told Hazel, when Hazel had broken the news of their marriage to her, 'Only the best is good enough for you, Ma, and Silas is the best.'

Hazel hadn't been able to disagree with that. Even now she could hardly believe she had found such happiness, been blessed with such love.

As she glanced at her new husband now and he looked back at her, she blushed at the promise she could read so clearly in his eyes, hoping that no one else could read it equally clearly.

There had been such a rush to arrange things, to put the house on the market and look for somewhere they could start their lives together, and to make all the other arrangements, that they had barely had any time at all together, alone. They had been lovers on less than a dozen occasions and each time Silas made love to her it increased her physical desire for him to such a pitch that now merely to look at him was enough to make her body positively hum with anticipatory delight.

She told herself sternly that it was a ridiculous way to feel at her age, but then Silas smiled at her, and she forgot all about her age, and remembered only that she was a woman and very much in love... very, very much in love.

'Time for us to leave, I think,' Silas whispered to her, adding, under his breath, 'Have I told you recently how much I'm aching to be alone with you?'

'Not for the last hour,' Hazel responded mischievously.

'You just wait,' he threatened her. 'You just wait until tonight...'

They were standing together, so wrapped up in one another that Hazel didn't even hear Katie approach until her daughter whispered in her ear, 'The way you two are looking at one another is almost making me blush.'

'We're just leaving,' Silas grinned at her, and then, looking tenderly at Hazel, added, 'That's if you're ready to leave, my love.'

'I'm ready,' Hazel told him huskily, while Katie laughed again and then hustled them both towards the door, claiming that now they really were embarrassing her.

HARLEQUIN ROMANCE®

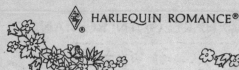

**Harlequin Romance
has love in
store for you!**

Don't miss next
month's title in

THE BRIDAL COLLECTION

A WHOLESALE ARRANGEMENT
by Day Leclaire

THE BRIDE *needed* the Groom.
THE GROOM *wanted* the Bride.
BUT THE WEDDING was *more* than
a convenient solution!

Available this month in
The Bridal Collection
Only Make-Believe
by Bethany Campbell
Harlequin Romance #3230

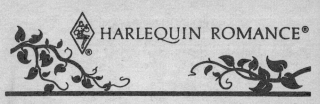

HARLEQUIN ROMANCE®

After her father's heart attack, Stephanie Bloomfield comes home to Orchard Valley, Oregon, to be with him and with her sisters.

Orchard Valley

Steffie learns that many things have changed in her absence—but not her feelings for journalist Charles Tomaselli. He was the reason she left Orchard Valley. Now, three years later, will he give her a reason to stay?

"The Orchard Valley trilogy features three delightful, spirited sisters and a trio of equally fascinating men. The stories are rich with the romance, warmth of heart and humor readers expect, and invariably receive, from Debbie Macomber."

—Linda Lael Miller

Don't miss the Orchard Valley trilogy by Debbie Macomber:

VALERIE   Harlequin Romance #3232 (November 1992)
STEPHANIE   Harlequin Romance #3239 (December 1992)
NORAH   Harlequin Romance #3244 (January 1993)

Look for the special cover flash on each book!

Available wherever Harlequin books are sold.   ORC-2

HARLEQUIN 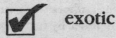 PRESENTS®

is

- ☑ exotic
- ☑ dramatic
- ☑ sensual
- ☑ exciting
- ☑ contemporary
- ☑ a fast, involving read
- ☑ terrific!!

Harlequin Presents—
passionate romances
around the world!